THE
Story OF US

**Based on the Hallmark Channel Original Movie
Written By Tracy Andreen and Deborah Jones**

TERI WILSON

Table of Contents

Chapter One

Looking back, Jamie Vaughn should have realized something was amiss on that cool February morning as she navigated the cobblestone streets of Waterford, Oregon's charming business district. All the signs were there—another vacant storefront, the cracks in the sidewalk that had lingered for months without being repaired, the suspiciously short line at the corner coffee shop.

But Jamie didn't notice any of those things.

With her favorite polka dot dress swishing around her legs and her cat carrier slung over her shoulder, she couldn't help seeing her hometown as she always had. The duck statues she loved so much—a mama trailed by four tiny ducklings—were lined up in a neat row on the wooden footbridge of the walking trail. A puppy romped playfully at the end of its leash in the crosswalk by the pizza parlor. Preschoolers in bright coats and knitted beanies held onto a walking rope as their teachers led them to the nearby park.

It was the same Waterford she'd known and loved her entire life, since she herself had been one of those fresh-faced preschoolers. So maybe, just *maybe*, she had a tendency to look at the business district through rose-colored glasses. Was that really so bad, though?

In this case, yes. Yes, it was.

If she'd stopped long enough to take a closer look at her surroundings, maybe she wouldn't have been caught so off-guard by what came later that day. But she didn't stop. She kept right on following the cobblestone path all the way to her bookshop, hands buried in the pockets of her red swing coat and rose-tinted glasses firmly in place.

A tiny meow came from the cat carrier as Jamie unlocked the frosted-glass door to the shop and stepped inside. Eliot, her orange tabby, never missed a day of work and liked to announce his arrival to the white French country bookshelves and the faux cherry blossom tree that loomed over the best-sellers table. As per usual, neither responded.

Jamie deposited the purple carrier onto the sales counter and gave Eliot's pink nose a gentle tap through one of its mesh windows. His bright gaze followed her as she made her way beneath one of the store's big arched walkways—with crown molding as white and frothy as icing on a wedding cake—to the inside of the square check-out area.

She unzipped the top of Eliot's bag.

Meow.

Eliot popped his furry orange head out of the cat carrier and cast an evaluating glance at his surroundings. He took his job as an official book-shop cat quite seriously.

"Oh, hello." Jamie smiled at him and was re-warded with a rumbling purr in response.

She scooped him up and lifted him out of the bag. "It's a beautiful day to sell books. Isn't it, Eliot?"

He blinked, which Jamie took as a yes. After all, wasn't every day a good day to sell books? Of course it was, particularly if you were a feline named after T. S. Eliot.

"Yes, I agree." Jamie nodded and released Eliot to pad along the smooth white countertop, weaving around vases of fragrant pink roses and waterfall orchids.

Many people didn't know T. S. Eliot's poems had been the inspiration for the musical *Cats*, but Jamie did. Just as she knew that Marcel Proust's *Remembrance of Things Past* was the longest novel ever written and that *First Impressions* was the original title of Jane Austen's beloved clas-sic *Pride & Prejudice*. Someday, she hoped to be a published author herself. Every now and then, she liked to imagine what her name might look like printed on one of the volumes that lined her bookshop's shelves.

Books were Jamie's thing; her one true love. Other than Eliot, of course. And her bookshop, which was aptly called True Love Books & Cafe. The name hadn't actually been Jamie's creation, but it fit. It always had.

She tossed her keys into the antique china dish where she usually kept them and got to work readying the shop for business. By the time she'd gotten the sales software up and running, watered all the flowers and checked to make sure there were plenty of iced sugar cookies, scones and Valentine cupcakes arranged on the covered crystal cake stands in the café section of the store, her first customer was already browsing the classics section.

Jamie had known Alex Lopez for years, although his tastes usually ran more toward the Stephen King end of the spectrum than any of the books he was currently contemplating. How many times had she had to remind him True Love was a romance bookstore before he'd finally stopped coming by in search of the kind of books that would have given her nightmares for days?

"Hi, Alex, what's up?" She cast him a curious glance as he picked up a hardcover copy of *The House of Mirth*—a special commemorative edition with the title spelled out in elegant gold script.

"Oh hey, Jamie. I was trying to figure out a good book to give Taylor for Valentine's Day." He studied the book's cover, brow furrowing. "She likes romantic comedies. I figure mirth is funny, right?"

Jamie paused. Where to start?

"Yes, it is. Um, and Edith Wharton is one of the greatest authors of all time. First woman to win a Pulitzer for literature," she said.

But she couldn't let the poor guy walk out of the shop thinking he'd just bought his girlfriend the literary equivalent of *When Harry Met Sally*. She held up a finger. "But in this case, 'mirth' is ironic."

Alex's face fell. "Oh."

Jamie picked up a copy of Shakespeare's *Much Ado About Nothing* from the same display table—also hardcover, embellished with hearts and cupids below the title. She held it up as if it were a sparkly new toy. "Also romantic, but much funnier and, spoiler alert, a happy ending."

Relief washed over Alex's face.

Until Jamie continued, because she just couldn't seem to stop herself when it came to books. "Although, if you want her crying on your shoulder about the importance of following your heart when it comes to true love, then *House of Mirth* it is."

Alex held one book in each hand, his attention flitting back and forth between them, weighing the benefits of a Valentine gift that served up laugher versus feels.

Better him than me.

"Happy deciding!" Jamie grinned.

Being single had its benefits, even during this month of hearts and flowers. The last thing Jamie needed was a Valentine. What she needed was a cure for her recent bout of writer's block. And maybe a chocolate raspberry mocha...with whip.

But a significant other? Nope. Been there, done that, got the T-shirt. Never again.

Alex, however, proved himself completely devoted, because mere seconds after their exchange, he turned up at the register with *both* books. Maybe he was simply hedging his bets. Either way, Jamie thought it was sweet—doubly so.

He set the books on the counter and slid them toward her. "You are a lifesaver."

"Well, I hope she likes them." She placed his purchase in a crisp white bag decorated with the True Love logo and smiled.

"Thank you, Jamie." Alex heaved a sigh of relief.

Definitely hedging his bets.

"Of course," she said. "Bye."

"Bye." He gave her a wave as he headed toward the shop's door, passing Lucy Baxter, Jamie's sole employee, on his way out.

"Hey, Luce." Jamie felt her smile widen.

Lucy managed True Love's small café and helped out with other odds and ends as needed, but she was more than just an employee. In the three years they'd been working together, she'd become Jamie's closest friend and confidante—

aside from Jamie's aunt, Anita Vaughn, who owned the business district's only flower shop.

Lucy tossed a stack of mail onto the sales counter and jammed a hand on her slender hip. "Did you know Lennox Music closed?"

"What?" Jamie blinked. "When?"

"I don't know. I just saw the place is empty, and there's a 'closed for business' sign on the front door." Lucy shook her head, sending her loose cinnamon brown curls swinging.

"That is the third business on this block since the beginning of the year." Jamie bit her lip and tried her best to ignore the fact that there wasn't a single customer in the store at the moment. Her charming little bookshop suddenly seemed cavernous.

And excruciatingly empty.

Lucy arched a brow. "Four, if you count Cassidy's Candles in December."

"What is going on?" Business had been a little slow lately, but Jamie had managed to convince herself there was nothing to worry about. Because there *wasn't*. People loved books, and True Love was practically a Waterford institution.

But four businesses closing up shop in less than three months' time wasn't a good sign. Not at all.

Jamie felt sick all of a sudden. Even the raspberry mocha she'd been dreaming about held little appeal.

She took a deep breath as she sifted through

the mail Lucy had brought in. Everything would be fine. Of course it would. Since True Love was a romance-focused bookstore, February was always their busiest month. Any day now, business would start booming.

And surely other shops would move in to fill the empty storefronts. The business district was Waterford's crown jewel—a little slice of cobblestone heaven. Who would rather shop someplace slick and impersonal like Portland when they could soak up the rich history of a place that had remained virtually unchanged since 1902?

No one with any sense, that's who.

But when Jamie unfolded the light blue flier nestled among her bills and junk mail, she had a horrible feeling that things were about to get worse instead of better.

"What?" she muttered, heart pounding as the innocent-looking slip of baby blue shook in her hands.

The flier was from the City of Waterford, notifying shop owners of a special town council meeting.

To discuss business district project by Ridley Property Development.

She read the words once...twice...three times, until the initial shock wore off. Then her heart seemed to sink straight to the soles of her red patent-leather kitten heels. Property development companies didn't move into historical districts to help preserve the past. They moved in to tear things down and build something else.

Something bigger and supposedly better; something shiny and new.

But where would that leave True Love Books?

A lump formed in Jamie's throat as she looked around her very lovely, very empty store and realized the truth. This shop she'd adored for as long as she could remember might be in trouble. *Real* trouble.

Rose-colored glasses could only do so much.

Fortunately, Jamie had never been one to wallow.

Her usual sense of optimism might have taken a hit with the surprise appearance of the horrid blue flier, but she had no intention of hiding among her books and waiting for the situation to go from bad to worse. In this one instance, her lack of customers was a good thing, as it gave her a chance to get out of the shop and do a little investigating while Lucy kept an eye on True Love Books.

She went door to door, up and down the sun-dappled sidewalks of the business district in a furious whirl of polka dots and clicking heels. For a moment, she'd been tempted to head straight to her aunt's flower shop, but then she'd thought better of it. Her aunt was almost like a second mother, especially since Jamie's parents had packed up and moved away from Waterford in their new RV. But there was no reason to alarm Aunt Anita until she had a better idea of what they might be up against.

Which turned out to be *a lot*. Or at least, it certainly seemed that way.

By the time Jamie finally stepped up to the door of Anita's Flowers, she had a sneaking suspicion the entire business district was in serious danger. Even the heady scent of pink parfait roses and blush-hued peonies failed to cheer her up. She closed her eyes and took a deep inhale, lingering outside her aunt's shop for a moment. Row upon row of cut flowers arranged into bouquets in buckets of water flanked the entrance, and hanging baskets of lush ferns and ivy swayed overhead. The names and prices of the blooms were all written by hand in tiny chalkboard print. Ever since Jamie had studied French back in high school, the corner boutique had reminded her of one of the charming flower stands that dotted the streets of Paris in her textbooks. The business district's cobblestone streets added to the old-world flair, but who knew how much longer those would last?

Jamie tightened her grip on the offensive flier as she pulled open the shop's glass door and the tinkling of delicate bells announced her arrival.

Her aunt looked up from a potted violet plant and smiled. "There's my favorite niece."

Not for long. Ugh, Jamie hated being the bearer of bad news. But the fact that she was Aunt Anita's *only* niece probably cemented her status as favorite.

"Your parents Skyped me last night. From Winnipeg!" Anita chattered away as she wiped her hands on her ivory linen apron and strode behind the counter. Her hair was in its standard loosely curled bob, and she wore a crisp pink button-down shirt with dark jeans. Aunt Anita had the same kind eyes as her sister, Jamie's mom, which always made Jamie feel a little bit less lonely—especially since her mom and dad had embarked on their big cross-country retirement trip six months ago.

Anita shook her head and let out a soft laugh. "I swear, they're going to put a hundred thousand miles on that RV by the end of the year if they…"

Her voice drifted off once she met Jamie's gaze. Anita stared at her for a beat, smile fading.

Note to self: work on my poker face.

"What is it?" her aunt said.

A huge cluster of red heart-shaped balloons bobbed behind Anita's head, making her sudden frown seem even more at odds with the cheery surroundings. February was also the busiest month of the year for Anita's Flowers. Jamie's aunt had spent weeks already preparing for Valentine's Day. Pink and red decorations covered just about every surface, from romantic Hallmark

Valentine cards to glittery gift bags and pink carnations.

So. Many. Carnations.

It was lovely, really—if you were into the whole romantic hearts and flowers thing, which Jamie definitely was. Just not the actual *romance* part of the equation. Or at least, not for her. But why was she thinking about her love life, or lack thereof, at a time like this?

She slapped the flier onto the counter for her aunt to see.

Anita's eyes grew wide. "When did you get this?"

"This morning. And I checked—every shop in the business district got one too." Every single store. What were they planning on doing? Mowing down the entire neighborhood? "I'll bet if you check your mail, you have one."

Anita gathered her stack of mail from the end of the counter and flipped through its contents. Sure enough, a blue flier identical to the one Jamie had received was tucked among her other, less-intimidating mail.

It trembled in Aunt Anita's hand as she unfolded it. "What do you think this means?"

Jamie took a deep breath. "I guess we'll find out at the meeting."

She read the bold print on the page one more time, just in case the letters had magically rearranged themselves into a more pleasant message.

Nope, no such luck. "But if this Ridley is a property *development* company..."

Anita sighed. "No, that can't be good news for any of us."

Chapter Two

S AWYER O'DELL STOOD AT THE head of the conference room in Ridley Property Development's modern downtown high-rise in Portland, Oregon, and advanced his PowerPoint presentation to the final slide. An animated rendering of his design spun across twin flat-screen televisions, showing every detail of his plans for the Waterford business district.

Correction—his *current* plans. This elaborate architectural plan was technically a re-design, his second attempt to please the higher-ups at Ridley. Which was probably why he was sweating beneath his pressed button-down shirt and tailored dress slacks, although from the pleased expression of the woman sitting at the head of the table, he didn't have much to worry about. All the late nights bent over his graphics tablet, sketching until his hand ached, had been worth it.

He was nailing this!

"So, as you can see, we will turn the Waterford business district into a mixed-use space, which will drive revenue for the entire town." Sawyer paused, giving his client a chance to take everything in as the animated slide slowed to a stop.

He glanced down at the architectural model in the center of the conference table while he waited. The miniature building had taken him weeks to get just right. All the effort had been worthwhile, though. It was a perfect replica of his design, from the multiple floors of industrial-style loft apartments that topped the structure all the way down to the retail space at the street level. He'd even managed to find tiny trees that looked almost exactly like the hemlocks and Douglas firs that lined the streets in Waterford.

That particular detail had been important to Sawyer. Over a decade had passed since he'd set foot in his hometown, but he remembered it as clearly as if it had been yesterday—soft, damp earth beneath his feet, the cool, and fresh scent of pine needles and trees so lush and green that he'd never seen anything like them, before or since.

He remembered more, too. He remembered how quaint and cozy the old houses in Waterford felt, tucked beneath the shadow of one of the most ancient cedar forests in the Pacific Northwest. He remembered learning to toss pizza dough high in the air at his first summer job. He remembered Sundae Madness at his favorite ice cream stand by the lake.

He remembered sharing those sundaes with Jamie Vaughn. She'd been his high school sweetheart, his very first love.

Since his underwhelming breakup with Sarah a few months ago, he'd even wondered if Jamie might have been his *only* love. But he'd chalked that thought up to the simple fact that he'd been neck-deep in Waterford nostalgia lately. It was normal to feel a bit sentimental while working on a project for his hometown, right?

"I like the adjustment," Dana Sutton, Vice President of Ridley Property Development, said with a nod, dragging Sawyer's thoughts back to the present—back where he was supposed to be. Where he *wanted* to be. "I think the Waterford Council will, too."

He breathed a triumphant sigh of relief. "Thank you."

Dana angled her head toward him, the blunt edge of her smooth blond bob skimming the collar of her white power suit. "Sawyer, how many projects have you done for Ridley? Five?"

He gestured toward his PowerPoint presentation. "If you pick this one, seven."

She nodded. "Seven. Impressive. I'm going to let you in on a little secret." Dana stood, striding past the conference room windows and their sweeping views of Portland down below. Sawyer followed her, because he supposed it was the right thing to do.

"The Waterford Project isn't secured yet," she said without bothering to turn around, as she clearly knew he'd be right on her heels. "It will be. Which is where you come in."

Dana slowed down enough for him to fully catch up.

"Me?" He started to feel uncomfortably warm again. He'd done his part—*more* than his part, technically. This was the second full set of designs he'd come up with.

"You're from Waterford," Dana said. "A point you made in your initial presentation."

Behind her, the Willamette River glittered jade green as it snaked its way through downtown Portland. Sawyer could see the snow-capped peak of Mount Hood in the distance, looming over the city he hoped would soon become his permanent home.

He wasn't a kid anymore—he'd just turned thirty-five. He'd had enough of crisscrossing his way all over the country. He wanted a home. A *life*. If he could just get a permanent position at Ridley rather than continuing on as a freelance architect, he might be able to make that happen.

"I am..." He nodded, wondering where this conversation could possibly be headed. So far, it didn't yet sound like the permanent job offer he wanted.

"That's going to help us when it comes to persuading the community." She beamed at him as if he was the answer to all of her problems.

She wasn't actually suggesting that he *go* to Waterford, was she?

Sawyer shook his head. "Hold on, Dana. I haven't been back in a very long time. And besides, I'm just the architect."

"But you could be more," Dana said. Yep, she was definitely suggesting a trip back home. Her enthusiasm almost made Sawyer wonder if she had a suitcase already packed for him, ready to go. "Here's your opportunity. The Waterford Council wants us to present our designs in a couple days before they take an initial vote next week."

If the vote was scheduled for next week, he'd only have to spend a few days in Waterford. But it had been ages since he'd set foot there. No way could he effectively sway the vote.

Dana seemed to think otherwise, though. "We've secured several properties already, but their sales are contingent on this project going to the next step. Help Ridley take that next step, and we can talk about bringing you in-house."

Sawyer opened his mouth to protest, then promptly closed it when he fully absorbed what she was saying. A permanent job at Ridley—exactly what he'd been hoping for.

Finally.

"So, no more per-project bids?" he asked, just

to clarify. After years of freelancing, it almost seemed too good to be true.

"How does that sound to you?" Dana smiled.

"That sounds great." Count him in. He'd do pretty much anything for a real job with real benefits. Something that would let him settle down in a real *home*. He had so many frequent flyer miles that he could've probably flown to the moon and back for free. First class.

"Good." The matter all settled, Dana nodded.

Sawyer wished he shared her confidence that his presence in Waterford would make a legitimate difference in the council's decision. What was he supposed to do—dust off his old letter jacket and remind all the locals that back in high school, he'd been crowned homecoming king? As marketing strategies went, it wasn't exactly a solid one. Besides, shouldn't his architectural plan be good enough to stand on its own merits?

But he'd make it work. Sawyer's closest friend, Rick, still lived in their hometown, so at least he'd have a comfortable place to stay, plus a respected local business owner to vouch for him. Towns that had been on the map for a while weren't always keen to roll out the welcome mat for real estate developers. Having Rick on his side couldn't hurt.

Sawyer had his work cut out for him, hometown connections or not. He could do this, though. He had to. Living out of a suitcase and working on projects all over the country was beginning to wear on him. He'd spent the last three Christmases in three different cities, and he wasn't sure he could even name them off the top of his head. He just needed to get to Waterford, convince the council to approve his plans for the redesign and then he could hightail it back to Portland.

Permanently.

Besides, it was only a few days out of his life. How hard could it be?

After breaking the news about the town council meeting to Aunt Anita, Jamie returned to True Love Books and did her best to put on a happy face. She unboxed the latest shipment of romance novels and put together a new Valentine's Day display, complete with paper flowers she and Lucy had made one night while sharing a bottle of rosé. They'd used pages from vintage books to make the petals, and the end result was a dreamy bouquet of words, perfect to accompany the new selection of romantic reads.

Even Jane Eyre roses weren't enough to make her forget about the blue flier tucked into the pocket of her dress, though. She kept taking it out and reading it again, just in case she'd missed some crucial detail.

None of this escaped Lucy's notice, of course.

The first few times Jamie succumbed to the urge to re-read the flier, Lucy didn't say anything. She polished the glass cake stands on the bookshop's café counter until they shone and busied herself with arranging pink-frosted cupcakes into a perfect pyramid, until she apparently could no longer hold her tongue.

"Maybe it won't be that bad?" she ventured, peering over Jamie's shoulder at the paper in her hand. Jamie had unfolded and refolded it so many times that it was beginning to look like bad origami. "I mean, the flier only says they're discussing a project."

Jamie turned to face Lucy and finally released the sigh she couldn't hold in any longer. "This happened a few years ago in Tanner Falls. Some developers came in and said they were going to do some 'improvements.'" Good grief, she was using air quotes. *Caution: now entering full rant mode.* "They wiped out all of the stores in the business district and then built them back up to look like something out of an H. G. Wells novel."

Lucy's eyes lit up. She'd always been a big fan of *The Time Machine.* Jamie sort of wished she had one of those, so she could go back to this morning and ignore her stack of mail entirely.

She held up a preemptive finger. "And not one of the cool ones."

They weren't talking *The Time Machine.* The developers had gone completely *War of the Worlds* crazy on poor Tanner Falls. It was almost unrecognizable. People who'd been in business for years no longer had a place in the trendy, new version of a town that no longer resembled itself.

"Well, if they do go forward with something like that, they at least have to buy you out." Lucy gave her a tentative smile.

She had a point. Still, Jamie's passion for her bookstore went way beyond the financial ramifications of being forced to close up shop. "But I'd still lose the store, and I've dreamed about owning this place since I worked here in high school. It's the reason I fell in love with reading and writing and storytelling. I don't want another store. I want True Love."

This place had been a haven for Jamie, her own personal paradise, for as long as she could remember. She'd been just a little girl the first time she'd walked through True Love's door, but the comfort of being surrounded by all those love stories was a feeling she'd never forget. Mr. Ogilvy, the prior owner, used to let her go there after school every day and read for hours. The first chapter book she'd finished, cover to cover, had been a beautifully illustrated hardback edition of *Little Women*. She could still remember the smell of its pages and the soothing weight of it in her hands, as if she'd been holding onto a whole new world of happy-ever-afters.

As soon as she'd turned sixteen, she'd begged Mr. Ogilvy for a job. She'd loved working at True

Love so much back then, she would've done it for free.

She *still* would, if not for pesky little details like her mortgage, groceries, utilities and Eliot's premium cat food. Only the best for her favorite ginger! No offense to Prince Harry, always a close second.

"Come on." Lucy took her by the wrist and began dragging her away from her Valentine's display.

Jamie lost her grip on the blue flier, and it floated toward the floor. Eliot, ever vigilant, did a little butt wiggle and then pounced on it.

Jamie groaned in protest, but Lucy was relentless. She grabbed Jamie's red coat and flung it at her, all the while maintaining a firm grip on her arm. "I know something that's going to make you feel better."

Doubtful...*highly* doubtful.

But she didn't have much of a choice, and honestly, Jamie was up for anything that might get her mind off of real estate developers, even if only for a minute or two. So she shrugged into her coat and let Lucy steer her toward the set of French doors at the back of the store that led to the courtyard behind True Love Books.

She breathed a little easier once they were outside. The courtyard was one of Jamie's favorite places in all of Waterford, not only because it had been her own creation, but because at its center stood the oldest tree in the business district.

The Oregon ash was over two hundred years old, with a trunk so thick that Jamie couldn't even wrap her arms all the way around it. She'd been reading books beneath the shade of its branches since she'd first learned how to decipher words on a page—for so long that the tree had become a loving symbol. Not just of Waterford's past, but of the promise of its future, as well.

That tree was timeless.

Jamie's first order of business after she'd taken over True Love Books was to clear out the area around the old ash tree and make it into a wonderland of twinkle lights, lush potted ferns and cozy café tables. Ballet-pink roses from Anita's Flowers decorated every surface, floating in glass bowls. The overall effect was like something out of a fairytale—just what Jamie had been hoping for.

"Is that Jason?" She peered through a cluster of greenery at an Asian man in his late twenties, sitting at one of the tables opposite a pretty young woman whose dark hair was twisted into stylish updo.

They were holding hands, and something about Jason's dapper coat and tie, coupled with the way he was reaching into his jacket pocket with his free hand, made Jamie think something special was about to go down.

"Uh-huh. He met Lisa in the travel section last year," Lucy whispered. "And I think he's going to propose!"

She pulled Jamie closer to her side and they crouched further out of view.

"I think you're right." Jamie held her breath as Jason rose from his chair and then bent down on one knee.

Should they be watching this? Maybe not. But Jamie couldn't resist a True Love proposal. Lucy knew her so well. This was indeed the one thing that was sure to lift her spirits. Her eyes filled with unshed, happy tears—

Until someone spoke directly into her ear, completely spoiling the ambiance. "What are we looking at?"

Jamie and Lucy both flinched.

Busted.

Jamie glanced over her shoulder, heart pounding a mile a minute. Rick Turner—friend, local chef and fellow busybody—was crouched right behind them, grinning.

"Rick!" Jamie whisper-screamed at him.

He laughed. "What?"

"Shhhh!" Lucy give his shoulder a playful swat, which was completely useless since Rick had been a defensive lineman in college and still somehow maintained his football player physique, despite his penchant for rich Italian cuisine.

"There's a proposal," Jamie explained under her breath, turning her attention back to the courtyard so she wouldn't miss the good part.

Just in time! Jason opened a red velvet ring

box to reveal a glittering diamond solitaire, and Lisa gasped, pressing her hands to her heart. The look on Jason's face was so tender, so full of hope and promise, that for a second, Jamie was tempted to re-think her recent decision to stop dating.

But not quite. She was perfectly content with just Eliot and her books, thank you very much. If that made her sound like a spinster from a Jane Austen novel, then so be it.

Lisa, on the other hand, seemed ready to sprint down the aisle. She beamed at Jason and broke down in tears as she gave him her answer. "Yes."

"Awwww," the eavesdroppers all said in unison.

Seriously, though. They should probably make themselves scarce so Jason and Lisa could celebrate in private. Jamie tugged on Lucy's sleeve and they tiptoed back through the French doors into the bookstore, with Rick following on their heels.

Jamie wasn't sure why Rick had stopped by, but she had a definite feeling it didn't have anything to do with re-stocking the baked goods in True Love's café.

"How many proposals does that make?" Lucy said as they passed the wall near the back of the store that was thoroughly covered with pink roses. It was the shop's most Instagrammed spot.

"Four since I bought this place." Warmth filled Jamie's chest. Moments like this reminded her just how special True Love was, not just to her, but to the entire community of Waterford.

"This shop really is a lucky charm for love." Rick cast a quick glance at Lucy and then looked away before she noticed. Poor guy.

"Ooh, I'm going to use that." Jamie pointed at him. Not a bad catchphrase, although the fact that Rick had been harboring a secret crush on Lucy for nearly a year without making any visible progress didn't exactly bode well for the whole good luck charm theory. It would help if he would simply tell Lucy how he felt.

Obviously.

"Which brings me to..." Rick pulled a red card from behind his back and held it up for them to see.

Jamie read the white cursive letters swirling just below a rendering of a heart-shaped dinner plate. "'Recipe for Love?' It's...a cooking class? For Valentine's Day?"

Lucy plucked the card from Rick's hand and studied it. "Not all of us are on a romantic time out."

"Hiatus," Jamie corrected.

Hiatus just had a better ring to it than *time out*, like it was a voluntary thing and not some kind of punishment. Which it totally wasn't. Her dating hiatus was working out quite well. She should've tried it years ago after her breakup with Sawyer O'Dell.

Lucy rolled her eyes, clearly unimpressed either way. "My boss, the incurable romantic who owns a romantic bookstore while actively avoiding romance. Do you see the irony here?"

Rick laughed, and Jamie glared at him. Seriously? He was mocking her when she knew his deepest, darkest secret?

"Is this for couples only?" Lucy pulled a face. She definitely wasn't part of a couple, which made it even more frustrating that Rick couldn't bring himself to confess his feelings for her.

Jamie had come close to telling her about a million times, but Rick had sworn her to secrecy. Besides, she generally liked to limit her meddling to eavesdropping on couples getting engaged in her courtyard.

Still, it was just so obvious. How Lucy had gone this long without figuring it out was a complete and total mystery. Maybe if Lucy read more Agatha Christie and less H. G. Wells, she would've picked up on a clue and realized that Rick worshipped the ground she walked on.

"No, no, no. All sorts of singles will be there." Rick spread his arms open wide. "Including yours truly."

Okay, maybe they were finally getting somewhere.

"Yeah, but you're teaching, so you don't count," Lucy said, handing the invitation back to him.

Then again, maybe not.

"He counts," Jamie blurted out.

But it was too late. Lucy was already darting

toward the café counter to help a customer eye-balling the cupcakes. Darn her and her excellent work ethic.

"Thanks," Rick muttered with a sigh.

"*Cooking class?*" Jamie shook her head.

She was trying her best to be supportive, she really was, but things were getting ridiculous. This new Valentine's cooking class was just the latest in a long string of restaurant events he'd manufactured for the sole purpose of spending more time with Lucy. Last month, it had been a New Year's Eve champagne tasting. The month before, he'd taught a gingerbread workshop. At the rate things were going, Waterford would soon become an entire town of cooking and lifestyle influencers.

"Just ask her out directly," Jamie said in the same voice she used when reprimanding Eliot.

Rick was an incredibly talented chef and a good-looking guy—literally tall, dark and handsome. More importantly, he was kind and thoughtful, with a great sense of humor. All of which made his staggering lack of confidence in the dating department wholly baffling.

He cast a longing glance at Lucy as she pre-pared a flavored latte, executing a perfect heart in the foam. "What if she says no?"

What if she says yes?

"Then you'll know," Jamie said. "Finally."

Rick let out another deep, weighty sigh. "I've got to go make some risotto."

Ah, the risotto excuse. Jamie knew it well.

She watched him march toward the exit, studiously avoiding meeting Lucy's gaze as he went. How much longer was this going to last? A man could only make so much risotto.

"Oh, boy," she mumbled to herself.

Why did she get the feeling that if unrequited love had a flavor, it would taste exactly like a creamy Italian rice dish with generous amounts of shaved Parmesan?

Later that night, Jamie wrapped her coziest cardigan around herself as she stood in front of the microwave oven in her kitchen, watching her Lean Cuisine spin round and round. She would've killed for a plate of Rick's infamous risotto right then, but alas, the only thing she had on hand was a frozen dinner and a nice bottle of red. At least the Lean Cuisine was spaghetti, her favorite. She'd simply have to wait until the next time she ate at Rick's restaurant to dive into a plate of unrequited love.

It wasn't so bad, really. She loved quiet nights at home. Plus, her dream of becoming a novelist wasn't going to happen without spending some quality time crafting her prose. When the microwave dinged, she removed the plastic tray containing her meal and inhaled the yummy scents of oregano and marinara sauce. Right on cue,

Eliot appeared from out of nowhere and began rubbing against her legs.

Meow.

Honestly, his begging was shameless sometimes.

"Eliot. I *just* fed you." She speared a fork into the tiny pile of spaghetti and shuffled toward the dining room in her sweatpants. Eliot followed her but abandoned begging for food in favor of chasing after the pompoms on her slippers as she walked.

Jamie's laptop sat open on the dining room table next to a yellow legal pad and a pile of discarded balls of paper, each one representing a failed attempt at chapter one of a new manuscript. But the night was young. She still had plenty of time to make some real progress on a fresh story.

Jamie had been toying with an idea for a cozy mystery with a rom-com twist for days but couldn't seem to get going. It was beyond frustrating. She loved books. She *lived and breathed* them. How could writing one be such a struggle?

She took a sip of wine and looked over what she'd managed to type so far. It didn't take long.

<u>Love Can Be Murder</u>

Chapter One

Maria paced across the kitchen floor, eyeing her phone. She paused in front of it. Started pacing again. Another pause.

Should I call him? Was it too soon? Too late?

Jamie set down her wineglass, took a deep breath and added another sentence.

She let out a sigh.

Not exactly riveting. She frowned at the screen, deleted the sentence and tried again.

She exhaled.

Groundbreaking. Next, she should probably start working on the acceptance speech for her Pulitzer.

She jabbed at the backspace key until, yet again, a blank screen stared her in the face. Somehow it felt as if the little blinking cursor was mocking her. How did actual authors do this?

Maybe she just needed a little inspiration. Or maybe worrying about Ridley Property Development's plan for the business district was messing with her creative flow.

Her jaw clenched. Definitely the latter—yet another reason to turn up at the town council meeting and let them know exactly how she felt about any plans to overhaul Waterford's most charming neighborhood.

She closed the laptop forcefully, just shy of slamming it shut.

Take that, mean blinking cursor.

The book she'd started reading a few days ago was right there next to her half-eaten dinner, practically begging to be read—a cozy mystery with a strong, brilliant heroine who became an amateur sleuth after serving as a spy during World War II. Just the sort of can-do character who'd never let some horrible property developer ruin everything she held dear.

Jamie grabbed the novel and headed toward the living room. "Snuggle time on the couch it is."

Meow.

Eliot trotted after her, vocalizing his ardent approval of the sudden change in plans for the evening. Next to accompanying her to the bookshop and begging for people food, cuddling was his favorite hobby.

Jamie dropped onto the sofa and mentally scored another point on the tally in favor of her dating hiatus as Eliot curled into her lap and kneaded at her sweatpants with his front paws—"making biscuits," as Aunt Anita always called it. She smiled as he started to purr.

Less time spent on relationships doomed for failure meant more time for her only truly loyal male companion. If only he could help her come up with a plot for her novel and stop whatever disaster was awaiting the business district, he'd be perfect.

That was probably asking too much of a cat, though. Jamie would simply have to handle things on her own.

Chapter Three

SHORTLY BEFORE ELEVEN P.M., SAWYER wheeled his suitcase into the entrance of Rick's sleek contemporary-style house in downtown Waterford. After the meeting with Dana at Ridley, he'd tossed some things into a bag and headed straight out of the city. One of the wheels on his suitcase wobbled—probably from sheer exhaustion. It was a wonder his luggage had any fight left whatsoever after all the traveling Sawyer had done over the past several years.

Just a few more days.

All he had to do was stick it out until the town council vote, make a convincing pitch, get everyone on board, and then he'd be home free. No more travel. No more temporary design gigs. No more unpacked boxes stacked in the corner of his apartment in Portland. Once he was a full-time architect at Ridley, he could finally *buy* a place. A unit in the high-rise on the river. Or maybe a condo near the bike path and Tilikum Crossing. On warm-weather days, he'd walk across the bridge to Ridley's office. He might even throw away his suitcase.

But first, he had work to do, right in his hometown.

"It's about time you came back. I was scared you'd never show your face again after coming in last in fantasy football," Rick said, grinning as he led the way to the modern, open-concept kitchen and filled a glass of water at the sink. The faucet looked like brushed nickel, and the sink was oversized, perfect for a chef.

"Remind me next time not to draft a quarterback first." Sawyer parked his wheeled luggage and took a look around the space.

He'd never seen Rick's house in person before, and it wasn't at all what he'd expected. When he thought of Waterford, he pictured charming historic cottages with white picket fences and gingerbread trim. With its sharp edges and minimalist vibe, Rick's home was the polar opposite in every way. It suited him, though, especially the killer kitchen.

"I will do no such thing," Rick said. He took fantasy football almost as seriously as he'd taken playing the competitive sport in his college days.

"Nice." Sawyer nodded at the surroundings. The sectional sofa and padded ottomans in the living room managed to look both comfortable and stylishly masculine. Rick's taste had certainly become more refined since their Little League days. "Thank you for this, man. Really."

"It's the least I can do as many times as you've let me stay with you in Portland." Rick handed him the glass of water. "And Chicago."

"Don't forget Missoula." Sawyer raised his glass.

Rick laughed. "How could I forget Missoula?"

Even with a restaurant to run, Rick made time to visit, no matter where Sawyer landed on the map. And Sawyer had been grateful for it. Having a friend around made things less quiet in a strange new place. A little less lonely, especially after the break-up with Sarah.

Although perhaps the most telling thing about their break-up six months ago had been that the aftermath hadn't left Sawyer feeling any lonelier than usual. Instead he'd felt...

Nothing.

And there he was, feeling all sorts of things about a place where he hadn't set foot for fifteen years. It was strange being back. He'd been so young in Waterford, so grounded—absolutely certain about who he was and where his future was headed. He couldn't help but wonder how that younger version of himself would feel about the fact that he'd been away for so long.

He swallowed hard and pasted on a smile for his oldest friend. "Less than a week, I swear."

"Hey, it's all good." Rick sank onto a large ottoman and looked up at Sawyer with an uncharacteristic hint of worry in his gaze. "Enough time for me to get your opinion on a little situation I can't quite figure out."

Sawyer sat down on the sofa opposite him, all ears.

"Um. Okay." Rick took a deep breath. "There's a woman."

Sawyer bit back a smile. "There always is."

Rick was legendary for being popular with the ladies. Even in elementary school, girls fought for a place beside him at the lunch table.

"I'm serious this time," Rick said, and there was no denying the earnestness in his tone.

Sawyer nodded. "Okay, okay. What's the situation?"

"I can't quite"—Rick gave him a sheepish grin—"ask her out."

"What?" Sawyer's mouth fell open. "That is *not* the Rick I know."

"Because I like her. I really, really like her. We had that *kerpow* moment when we first met. You know what I'm talking about," Rick said.

"I do." Sawyer knew it well, even though he hadn't actually experienced a *kerpow* moment of his own in years. Not since high school, to be exact. He'd fallen head over heels for Jamie Vaughn the moment he first saw her reaching for the same book that he'd been looking for. *Kerpow*, indeed.

He took a gulp of his water. Again, being back in Waterford was messing with his head.

Meanwhile, Rick was still waxing poetic about his dream girl. "And I can't forget it. She liked me, too. I know she did."

"Why didn't you ask her out then?" This seemed like a no-brainer.

"I was dating Megan." Rick pulled a face.

"Megan." Wow. If memory served, she'd already had their wedding planned by the second date. Sawyer was fairly certain the wedding party included fourteen bridesmaids. "That disaster."

Rick sighed. "Thanks for reminding me."

"Never mind. Sorry." There was no sense revisiting past mistakes. Sawyer was all about moving forward. "You were telling me about..."

"Lucy. Yeah." Rick's face split into dopey grin. "But I made the classic mistake of letting too much time pass after we first met, and now I'm not sure if she only sees me as a friend, or..."

Sawyer burst out laughing. He just couldn't help it. "I can't believe the day has arrived when Rick the Romancer has met his match. Now when do I get to meet this girl?"

"Ah. Tomorrow night. I'm doing this Valentine's thing—a cooking class down at the restaurant, and Lucy said she'd come." There was the dopey grin again. Sawyer was suddenly very glad Dana had all but forced him to come for the town council vote. Seeing Rick reduced to a lovesick puppy was well worth the trip. "Do you think that you could...?"

"Count me in." He wouldn't miss it for the

world. "You know, just obviously don't expect me to cook anything edible."

Unpacked boxes labeled *kitchen* had been sitting around his apartment for nearly a year. Or was it two?

"Oh, I know better. No, no, no, I'm the chef." He pointed double finger guns at Sawyer. "You're the wingman."

Rick the Romancer needed a wingman. There truly was a first time for everything.

"Yes, chef." Sawyer nodded with exaggerated seriousness.

"Thanks."

"No problem." He smiled, and glanced out the window at the soft streetlights casting a luminous glow over the quiet streets below—streets where he'd first learned how to ride a bike without training wheels, where he'd played catch with his mom, where he'd walked his high school sweetheart home from school.

Why had he stayed away for so long? He hadn't intentionally turned his back on his hometown. It had just sort of it happened. He'd gone away to college and one year had turned into two, two into four. His mother had come up to Columbia during the holidays so they could spend Christmases in New York. After graduation, he'd been consumed by his work. Then his mom had moved across the country, and he hadn't had any reason to come back. Waterford had simply faded further and further into his past until it had become nothing but a memory.

He'd thought it had, anyway. Now he wasn't so sure. Sitting across from Rick, laughing and making plans, he didn't feel like he'd stepped into a memory.

He almost felt like he'd come home.

The following day was Tuesday, more commonly known throughout the book world as pub day. For as long as Jamie had worked at True Love Books—even back in high school—Tuesday had been the day of the week when newly published books became available to sell. She had no idea how or when this literary tradition first came to be, but it was very much a thing. Publishers large and small released their latest offerings on Tuesday mornings, just like clockwork. So of course it was Jamie's favorite day of the week.

Too bad the town council meeting was scheduled for lunchtime, ruining what should have been a perfectly lovely Tuesday. At least after the meeting, she'd have a better idea of what the developers had in mind. Until then, she'd just have to busy herself with celebrating all the new book birthdays and properly displaying her latest inventory.

She spent the morning unpacking boxes in

the storeroom and getting the new novels shelved. Eliot tiptoed behind her, pausing every so often to wrap his ginger tail around her leg, which Jamie liked to think of as a kitty hug. Lucy worked the sales floor, darting back and forth between the café counter and the sales register.

As Jamie headed to the back of the store for her third armload of hardbacks, Lucy was gift wrapping a journal for a customer doing some Valentine's Day shopping. But when Jamie rounded the corner, books in hand, she stopped short at the sight of a familiar, well-coiffed woman flipping through the pages of a Brontë novel near the paper flowers display.

Oh, no. She darted behind a corner and hid. What was Karen Van Horn doing at True Love Books?

Not her. Not now.

"Hi. Can I help you find something?" Lucy's voice rang like a bell from behind the sales counter.

Please say no. Please just go away. Jamie squeezed her eyes shut tight in a pathetic attempt to make herself invisible.

"You know, actually, I was hoping to catch Jamie," the woman said. "Is she here?"

Ugh.

She couldn't do this, not today, of all days. The pending town council meeting was a big enough thorn in her side. She couldn't handle dealing with her ex-boyfriend's mother. Jamie had broken up with Matt months ago. What could she and Mrs. Van Horn possibly have left to say to one another?

Maybe her romantic hiatus needed to broaden in scope to include not just prospective dating partners, but their family members as well.

Or maybe she was just a chicken. Possibly—probably—both.

"Um." Lucy's gaze flitted in Jamie's direction, and Jamie fled back to the storeroom like the chicken that she was.

Eliot batted a paw at her as she zipped past him. The tattletale.

"She is not," Lucy said awkwardly.

"Oh." Mrs. Van Horn sounded surprised. Obviously, she remembered that Jamie practically lived at True Love. "Do you know when she'll be back?"

"I'm sorry. I don't."

Thank goodness for Lucy.

Jamie sagged against the wall in relief. She wasn't foolish enough to believe she could hide from Matt's mother forever, but at least she could pull it off a little while longer. Today was going to be difficult enough without the added stress of a surprise visitor from her past.

Intellectually, Sawyer knew that not much had changed in Waterford since he'd left for college.

He had, after all, been poring over current blue-prints of the layout of the business district for weeks while working on the plans for Ridley's redesign. It wouldn't be an understatement to say he knew the neighborhood like the back of his hand. He was well aware that the dance school, the pizza parlor, the bike shop and numerous other old haunts of his were still right where he'd left them.

He also knew that more than a few businesses had either closed or were struggling, which was precisely why the town council wanted to over-haul the area. So when he took off from Rick's house Tuesday morning to explore the area on foot before the meeting, he knew exactly what to expect.

Still, seeing the old stomping grounds in per-son was a far different experience than reading about them on paper. He'd forgotten about the hanging flower baskets that dotted the streets with splashes of color every few feet. He'd also forgotten that the corner telephone poles had all been painted with bold abstract designs by the middle school art club. Little details, like the feeling of cobblestones beneath his feet and the sight of the line of brightly colored cruiser bikes in the bicycle stand on the corner of Main and 3rd Street—things that were impossible to see on a map or a grid—made him feel as if he'd stepped back in time to a season in his life when things were simpler. Slower. Maybe even happier.

In Waterford, strangers made eye contact and said hello. They smiled and made room for him on the sidewalk instead of staring down at their phones while they brushed past him. It had been a long while since he'd experienced that kind of small-town charm.

He passed a few vacant storefronts, and his throat grew thick. As much as he loved the nostalgia of Waterford, the business district was clearly past its prime. He knew this. It was the very reason he was there. But at the same time, it felt like an arrow to his heart.

Buck up. This is a business trip, not a stroll down memory lane.

He took a deep breath, refocused, and reminded himself what was at stake. His entire future depended on what happened over the course of the next few days, starting with the town council meeting this afternoon. He had to keep his head in the game.

A couple dressed in hiking boots and matching raincoats strolled past him, then paused to staple a poster to the telephone pole. It looked like a few of the other posters he'd seen around town already—advertisements for an upcoming Valentine-themed event called the Fire and Ice Festival. Sawyer had never heard of it before, so it must've been something new.

He shrugged one shoulder and moved on, reminding himself to regard the quaint community through a more neutral architect's eye. There was much room for improvement. As charming as it was, the area just wasn't self-sustaining anymore. Adding a mixed-use development could blend residential, commercial and cultural spaces into one area and create a pedestrian-friendly environment that would thrive. Waterford might lose some of its old-world charm in the process, but in the end, change would save the district.

But as he kept walking, his messenger bag slung over his shoulder, Sawyer's gaze landed on the shop at the street corner and he slowed to a halt. Three small café tables that looked like something straight out of an old-fashioned ice cream parlor sat on the sidewalk outside the store. Planter boxes overflowing with red and pink geraniums were perched on the windows. But the *pièce de résistance* was the faux cherry blossom tree sitting in a red pot beside the shop's door with delicate pink flowers climbing up the building's brick exterior and surrounding the entrance with artfully arranged cascading blooms.

The overall effect was breathtaking. Unapologetically romantic—and even prettier than it had looked in the photographs he'd studied for his designs. Sawyer had never seen anything quite like it, even though the shop itself was a place he'd visited many, many times.

True Love Books & Cafe. The swinging sign that spelled out the shop's name in swirling cursive letters was the same one that had hung beside the door back when Sawyer used to walk

Jamie Vaughn to work after school. Seeing it again after all this time made him smile.

He lingered on the threshold, tempted to take a look inside. A few minutes couldn't hurt. For old times' sake.

A bell tinkled overhead as he pushed the door open, announcing his arrival. But the sound might as well have indicated he was stepping back in time, because even though the bookshop had clearly been updated in the years he'd been away, simply breathing the air in the old building made him feel steeped in memory. He took a deep inhale, savoring the comforting scent of ink on paper with a touch of something else—warm vanilla, maybe—a unique fragrance he'd forever associate with young love.

With Jamie.

Even now, all these years later, he couldn't walk into a library or a used bookstore without thinking about the feeling of her hand in his or the graceful tilt of her head when she bent over a book, her blond hair falling over her shoulder in a smooth, glossy curtain.

He blinked. Hard. It was strange the way memory worked, wasn't it? It could catch you off guard at the oddest moments. When he opened his eyes, the first thing he noticed was an orange tabby cat lying on the sales counter, flicking its tail and gazing impassively at Sawyer.

A bookshop cat? Cute.

He took a tentative step toward the animal.

It blinked lazily at him, so he offered his hand and was rewarded with a loud purr as the kitty rubbed its cheek against his knuckles.

The cat was definitely new, as were the white-washed furnishings and bouquets of flowers that decorated nearly every surface. Painted mason jars filled with peonies and hollyhocks were tucked among the shelved books, and the old pink piano stood in the corner, piled high with hardbacks and a vase of white roses. *True Love* had always been a sort of monument to romance, hence its name. But since the last time Sawyer had spent any time there, someone had lovingly transformed the shop from its charming begin-nings to a breathtaking ode to love and literature. The architect in him was nearly as impressed as his inner hidden romantic.

He was ambling deeper into the shop, running his fingertips over a row of books down a narrow aisle, when a voice suddenly pulled him out of his memories and back to the present.

"Look out!"

Out of pure instinct, he reached up and caught a falling book before it hit him in the head. But it must have still knocked something loose inside him because when he glanced up, he was transfixed by the sight of a woman perched atop a rolling ladder staring down at him, wide-eyed.

Not just any woman, but *her*—Jamie Vaughn, his high school sweetheart.

"Good catch," she said with an unmistakable hint of wonder in her tone.

Sawyer would know that voice anywhere. He wasn't dreaming, was he? It was really Jamie.

Kerpow.

A wistful smile tipped her lips. "Sawyer."

He'd never experienced such a loss for words before, so he said the first thing that popped into his head. And since he'd unexpectedly found himself staring into the eyes of the girl who loved books more than anyone else he'd ever met, those words happened to be borrowed from William Shakespeare.

"'But, soft! What light through yonder window breaks?'"

"What?" She blinked, and he was suddenly acutely aware that Jamie wasn't a high school girl anymore. Her face was more angular now, giving more definition to those high, delicate cheekbones and porcelain complexion. Her adorably awkward teenaged frame had been replaced with willowy grace. Sawyer's favorite bookworm had grown into a beautiful woman while he'd been away.

His heart thumped hard in his chest. "It's *Romeo and Juliet.* You, uh, look like you're up on a balcony."

She didn't move. She just kept standing up there in her prim black cardigan and polka dot pencil skirt, staring down at him as if he'd arrived via time machine. It sort of felt like he had.

"There was no balcony," she said.

Sawyer tightened his grip on the book in his hands. Why was he sweating all of a sudden? "What?"

"In the story. She's just standing at a window. Everybody gets it wrong."

Sawyer knew better than to argue. Still, this unexpected little reunion wasn't progressing at all the way he'd always imagined it would. Not that he'd been planning, or even hoping, to see her while he was back in Waterford. The last he'd heard, she was thinking about moving to Texas. But he'd be a liar if he said bumping into her hadn't crossed his mind over the years. He'd just never considered he might botch Shakespeare when it finally happened.

He swallowed. "Oh."

"I'm sorry. Um. I'm just..." She deposited her armload of books onto the top shelf and climbed down the ladder so they stood face-to-face. "Completely thrown."

Had her eyes always been such a startling shade of blue?

"Yeah, so was I. I suppose I shouldn't be. This was always your favorite place." He couldn't believe she still worked there, though. How was it possible that everything in Waterford had changed and yet somehow, stayed exactly the same?

"Let's start again." She smoothed down her dotted skirt, and Sawyer couldn't help but smile because polka dots had always been her trade-mark. "Hi, Sawyer!"

"Hey, Jamie." He was beginning to feel like a kid again, walking his girl to work after school. "You dropped this."

He offered her the book that had nearly fallen on his head.

She took it, and her grin wobbled just a little. If he'd blinked, he would have missed it entirely.

"Thank you." She stared for a beat at the il-lustrated cover of the book's blue dust jacket.

It was only then that Sawyer noticed which flying novel he'd managed to narrowly avoid—*Persuasion* by Jane Austen. Oh, the irony.

Chapter Four

*J*AMIE HUGGED THE AUSTEN NOVEL to her chest while she made small talk with Sawyer. She had no idea what she was saying—at one point, she could have sworn she heard herself talking about Eliot's most recent hairball, but she couldn't be sure. Her thoughts were a complete blur. She'd been reeling since she'd first caught sight of him—Sawyer O'Dell, in Waterford, after so much time.

And she'd nearly conked him in the head... with *Persuasion!* Of all the books in the world, why did it have to be that one?

It was Jamie's favorite Austen novel. Sure, she loved Mr. Darcy from *Pride and Prejudice* as much as the next bibliophile—so much that she absolutely refused to choose which movie Mr. Darcy was the best. As far as Jamie was concerned, the more Darcys, the better.

But there was just something about Anne Elliot and Captain Wentworth from *Persuasion* that made her weak in the knees—perhaps because they went against the usual formula. They met and fell in love when they were young. Shortly after they got engaged, though, they broke up and Wentworth left to rise through the ranks in the Navy. When he returned seven years later, Wentworth and Anne were near-strangers. But, of course, they fell in love all over again, even amid a variety of humorous encounters and missed opportunities. Wentworth finally confessed his feelings to Anne in a beautiful letter where he told her, "You pierce my soul. I am half agony, half hope. Tell me that I am not too late..."

Those were undoubtedly the most romantic words Jamie had ever read. But having them pressed against her heart while trying to make polite conversation with Sawyer when she hadn't set eyes on him in fifteen years was more than she could take. Honestly, it was full-on, one-hundred-percent agony.

What was he doing here? His mom had moved away years ago, and he certainly wasn't in town to see Jamie. She hadn't heard from him at all since their breakup back when they were eighteen. Not a single word. He'd been her first love, but more importantly, her very first heartbreak. Sometimes she even wondered if the reason she hadn't been able to fully commit to a relationship with Matt was because deep down, she knew she'd never fully gotten over Sawyer.

But that was ridiculous. She'd moved on *long* ago. Still, she couldn't keep standing there, talking to Sawyer as if the past decade and a half hadn't happened. Not when he looked so handsome in a navy peacoat that suddenly seemed far too Wentworth-esque. And certainly not here, in a place that had so many shared memories for them.

"Why don't we go for a walk?" she blurted, interrupting Sawyer mid-sentence.

Not that he'd been saying anything important. Neither of them had managed to get past benign pleasantries such as talk about the weather.

"A walk?" He cocked his head. "Sure, that sounds nice."

Good. She needed air, and she definitely needed to get as far away from Jane Austen as possible.

She shoved the copy of *Persuasion* onto the nearest bookshelf and led him around the corner, past the blooming flower wall and out the French doors onto the smooth pavement of the courtyard. Thank goodness no one was busy getting engaged out there at the moment.

Sawyer glanced around at the twinkle lights woven through the latticework fencing and the elegant topiaries arranged in large potted plants. "I don't remember this courtyard."

Exactly. That was the entire point of ushering him outside. It was neutral territory—mostly, anyway. The cafe tables and sitting area hadn't existed back when Sawyer had been quarterback of the Waterford High football team.

He looked like he could still score a winning touchdown, though. The peacoat couldn't hide his broad, muscular shoulders. There were new crinkles around his eyes and the slightest touch of gray at his temples, but those little details just made him seem more manly. More grown up.

She averted her gaze to look at something that didn't make her heart feel like it was about to beat right out of her chest. "Oh, but you remember the tree, right? The tree was always here. In fact, they actually built the bookstore around it so they wouldn't have to take it down."

Sawyer tilted his head back to see the very top of the old Oregon ash. Its pale gray branches looked almost white against the clear blue sky. A muscle flexed in the corner of his chiseled jaw, and Jamie almost tripped over a fern.

She cleared her throat. "But yeah, this courtyard was completely overgrown. I talked Mr. Ogilvy into letting me clean it up a few years ago. And we're hoping to expand. Or I should say *were* hoping to expand."

Was she rambling? It felt like she was rambling.

"You *were*? But not anymore?" Sawyer arched a brow.

"Ah, it's a long story." Jamie kept walking, making a wide loop around the courtyard. "These developers are buying all of the land in the business district. And, I mean, you know they're just going to destroy everything."

Sawyer stumbled a little. "Destroy?"

She was getting ahead of herself. The town council meeting was still scheduled for later in the afternoon, and Jamie definitely intended to make her thoughts on the subject heard. She refused to believe all hope was lost already. "Well, it's not decided yet. But they're having a meeting later to see if they're going to move forward with the project. You know what business developers do, though. They just tear everything down and put up something hideous."

Sawyer slowed to a stop and frowned. "It might not be hideous."

Did it even matter what they built if it meant the end of True Love? "Well, I'm sure they will not leave my little bookstore unscathed."

"Your..." He glanced at the store and back at her. "Wait, you...you bought the bookstore?"

"Yeah. Oh, yeah." Had she not made that clear already? "I bought it a few years ago, just like I always said I would."

Did he not remember, or did he simply think that everyone moved away from their hometown and never looked back?

"I had no idea," he said, blinking rapidly before letting out a strangled-sounding laugh.

"Well, how would you? You've been gone for fifteen years." There. She'd said it. "Unless Rick tells you everything."

"Not that thing," he said under his breath.

She was a little stumped as to why he seemed so surprised. He'd just seen her on top of a ladder shelving new books. Did he really think she was still working part-time in the afternoons for Mr. Ogilvy?

"Well, enough about me." She pasted on a smile. "How are you? What are you doing back here?"

She was dying to know. Rick hadn't breathed a word about Sawyer coming back. And Sawyer's crisp blue dress shirt and the messenger bag that was currently slung over his shoulder kind of made it seem like this was more than simply a vacation—not that it seemed likely he'd come to visit on a whim after all this time.

"I...um..." His face went blank for a second, and then the chime of a cell phone had him reaching for his pocket. "Oh, excuse me. Hold on..."

Jamie nodded, wondering who would be calling him. Then she wondered why she cared as two bothersome words echoed in her consciousness: *romantic hiatus.*

Sawyer's brow furrowed as he glanced at the screen of his ringing iPhone. "Oh. Um, sorry. I have to..."

"Oh." Jamie nodded again while Sawyer held the phone to his ear. She couldn't seem to stop.

"Hey, Dana. Can you hold on just a second?"

Sawyer glanced up from his phone with an apologetic smile. "I have to take this."

Whoever Dana might be, she was clearly important to him. And that was perfectly fine. Jamie didn't even know Sawyer anymore.

Seeing him again had been nice, though. Not quite as agonizing as she'd originally feared.

"Of course," she said, shooing him off. "Yeah, go. It was great to see you again."

"Good to see you too. Bye." He was already walking away, practically sprinting toward the courtyard exit. "Hey, Dana. Yeah..."

He waved at her one last time before he disappeared.

"Bye," she said, and her heart gave a little squeeze.

Then she took a deep inhale, squared her shoulders and marched back inside her bookstore. This was nothing more than history repeating itself. Jamie had grown accustomed to saying goodbye to Sawyer O'Dell a long, long time ago.

Jamie put on a brave front when she went back to shelving books, but it would have been nice to have had some time to regroup after her high school sweetheart resurfaced out of the blue, quoting Shakespeare and acting like he'd just walked out of the pages of a Jane Austen novel. A break was definitely in order. Fifteen hours or so would have been nice—one for each year that had passed since Sawyer O'Dell had broken up with her the summer after their high school graduation.

Unfortunately, she didn't have fifteen hours to spare, since the town council meeting was scheduled to begin less than an hour after Sawyer left.

She shelved like a madwoman, channeling all of her confusion into getting the shiny new books perfectly displayed before it was time to close up and head to her aunt's flower shop so they could walk to the meeting together.

She debated whether or not tell Anita that Sawyer had dropped by...and ultimately decided against it. Anita had always loved Sawyer. *Everyone* loved Sawyer. But if she mentioned it, the fact that he was back in town would become a *thing*. And Jamie had already decided it definitely wasn't a thing. It was a non-thing, really. Sure, it had been nice to see him, but she had more important things to think about.

Namely, saving her bookstore.

The town council meeting was set to take place at the Waterford Community Center, an old church that had been converted into a theatre and meeting hall. With its tall steeple and arched stained-glass window, it had always been one of Jamie's favorite buildings in the business district. Even though the space hadn't served as a house of worship for thirty-some-odd years, it still carried the distinct, comforting aroma of candle wax, furniture polish and old hymnals. Light spilled in from the nave windows overhead, and every tiny sound echoed off the smooth oak floors.

As lovely as the old building was, Jamie hummed with nervous energy when she and Anita walked through the door. The turnout for the council meeting was huge. They were ten minutes early, and the foyer was already packed. A few of Anita's friends huddled in a group around the coffee station, and she peeled off to greet them while Jamie took in the architectural plans displayed on large easels around the perimeter of the room. A scale model of a hyper-modern superstructure that looked more like a spaceship than a building sat on a table beside a podium.

Jamie stared at it, aghast, until a nice-looking man in a sleek business suit and red power tie approached her.

He smiled. "It's Jamie Vaughn, right? With True Love Books?"

"And Cafe, yes." She nodded.

"Eric Duncan." He held out his hand. "I'm new to the city council, and the area."

"Nice to meet you, Councilman." Jamie shook his hand and smiled back at him.

"I'm glad you dropped by to see the designs for the development." He tipped his head toward the miniature spaceship.

Ugh.

"*Proposed* development," she corrected.

"Proposed development." He let out a soft laugh, and the corners of his eyes crinkled. He seemed nice, at least. Not like the sort of person who would want to tear down a bookstore. "We're hopeful it will generate some much-needed interest in the local business community."

"Well, what about the Fire and Ice Festival? It has drawn a lot of interest in the area and been very popular for the last three years," Jamie said.

Practically everyone in Waterford came out for the festival which was a street fair held in the heart of the business district in the days leading up to Valentine's Day. All the local businesses set up booths and the whole area was decorated with flaming heart-shaped torches and grand ice sculptures—hence the festival's name. In just three years, the Fire and Ice Festival had become a full-fledged Waterford tradition.

Eric nodded. Good. At least he'd heard of the event. "And I hope it continues to be, but we should consider all options."

"Sure. I just have a million questions." She could hear herself talking too fast, but Eric the Councilman was beginning to glance around, distracted, and she still had a lot to say. "Starting with what happens to the existing stores if this project goes through?"

Someone in the periphery called his name, and he cut her off. "I'm sorry, could you excuse me for a second?"

Then Eric and his power tie were gone before

she'd made any headway whatsoever. Super. She lifted her chin, determined. There had to be someone else influential she could talk to before the meeting commenced.

She peered into the crowd, searching for another member of the town council, but froze in place at the sight of a familiar chiseled face. Her breath caught in her throat.

Sawyer?

His gaze flitted toward her and they locked eyes for a moment across the packed room. Sure enough, it was Captain Wentworth himself, smiling and shaking hands with Councilman Eric.

"Hi," she mouthed, waving at him before she could stop herself.

Something strange was going on. What on earth was he doing at the town council meeting? And why would he possibly be interested in schmoozing with a local politician?

Sawyer broke away from his chat with Eric to head her way, and she breathed a sigh of relief. Maybe she'd finally get to the bottom of his sudden reappearance.

"Jamie!" He flashed her a crooked smile.

The dimple in his left cheek that she'd always loved so much was still right there, looking as boyish and charming as ever. Because of course it was.

She opened her mouth to say something witty yet probing, but before she could utter a word, Aunt Anita returned with a squeal.

"My goodness. Sawyer O'Dell?" Anita looked him up and down as if he were some kind of handsome mirage.

Sawyer's face split into a wide grin and he wrapped his arms around her. "Hello, Anita."

Jamie stood by awkwardly while they hugged and tried not to think about how Anita had doted on her the entire summer after graduation, determined to help mend Jamie's broken heart. There had been copious amounts of ice cream and trips to the Waterford animal shelter to bottle-feed orphaned kittens. Anita had been amazing, and by the start of Jamie's first college semester, she'd felt almost whole again.

Still, Anita had never once bad-mouthed Sawyer back then. And all those ice cream dates and kitten outings suddenly seemed forgotten...

Which was completely fine. *Jamie* was completely fine, thank you very much. She was over Sawyer O'Dell.

She grinned brightly at him, just to prove it. "So. Nothing for fifteen years and then I see you twice in one hour?"

"Um. Yeah." Sawyer glanced back and forth between Jamie and Anita, shifting his weight from one foot to the other and back again. He seemed a little uncomfortable all of sudden. Guilty, even. His bone structure, however, remained annoyingly perfect. "Well, I wasn't exactly sure how to broach the subject earlier..."

"Sawyer?"

His eyes cut to a woman dressed in an elegant white blouse and an expensive-looking black pantsuit who was sashaying toward them, intently focused on Sawyer.

"Are the designs ready to show?" she asked, completely ignoring Jamie and Anita's presence.

Sawyer nodded. "Yes. They are queued up."

Designs?

What designs?

Somewhere in the periphery, Jamie could see Anita nervously fidgeting. But she didn't dare drag her attention away from Sawyer and the strange woman, who she suspected might be named Dana.

"Excellent." The woman nodded, finally appearing to notice Jamie and Anita. Sure enough, a D-shaped charm hung from a delicate gold chain around her neck. "Hello. Are you local business owners?"

Jamie was too busy staring daggers at her to say anything, so Anita jumped in with an introduction. "Yes, we are. I'm Anita Vaughn from Anita's Flowers. And this is my niece..."

Jamie raised her hand. "Jamie Vaughn. True Love Books & Cafe."

She glanced at Sawyer. Beads of sweat were starting to break out on his beautiful forehead.

"Nice to meet you both." Dana's glossy blond bob swung as she spoke. "I hope you'll be as excited as we are about the vision we have in mind for the project."

"*Proposed* project," Jamie countered. She really wished she didn't have to keep saying that.

Dana gave a dismissive wave of her hand, clearly unconcerned with semantics. "I'm confident that Sawyer's designs will help persuade the council to go forward."

Sawyer's smile froze in place, and Jamie stared at him in complete and utter horror.

"Ready?" Dana smiled widely at Sawyer before heading for the podium.

He went still for a second, like a deer in headlights.

Jamie's entire body quivered with indignation. She crossed her arms as aggressively as she could. "*Your* designs?"

He glanced at Anita and then back at Jamie, wincing. "Yeah..."

And then, much to Jamie's annoyance, he fled. He beat a hasty path to the head of the room and started chatting with Dana and Councilman Eric while gesturing to the spaceship model.

Correction: *his* spaceship model.

"Are you all right?" Anita rested gentle fingertips on Jamie's elbow.

She wasn't all right. She wasn't fine anymore, either. Far from it.

How could she have been so blind? She really should have seen this coming. She'd asked Sawyer point-blank why he was in Waterford, and he'd never answered the question. He wasn't a Jane Austen hero at all. He could recite all the

Shakespeare he wanted, but that didn't mean Jamie knew him anymore. He was practically a stranger.

Sawyer laughed at something the councilman said and Jamie glared at him. "I guess we'll find out."

Chapter Five

AN HOUR LATER, JAMIE WAS back at True Love, sipping a latte so beautiful that it was more of a work of art than a simple coffee drink.

Either Aunt Anita had given Lucy a heads up about the Sawyer situation or her best friend intuition was simply really spot-on, because the moment Jamie crossed the threshold, Lucy was ready and waiting with a giant latte cup in each hand. Each of the drinks was topped with a perfect heart swirled into the foam—a feat that had taken Lucy *weeks* to perfect once Jamie had invested in a gorgeous stainless-steel espresso maker for the store. Now True Love sold more coffee drinks than the diner down the street.

People liked romance. They liked hearts swirled into their foam and visiting a shop that was as much a love letter to the community as it was a bookstore. But all of that would change if Sawyer got his way.

Jamie sipped her latte and pored over the details of the proposed Ridley project on her iPad while Lucy rang up customers. She'd been right to be worried about the plans for the redesign. The model of the spaceship building was slated to be the new centerpiece of Waterford's business district, and Ridley wanted to put it on the exact corner that True Love currently occupied.

"There you go. Enjoy!" Lucy said as she handed another of her frothy lattes to a customer, along with one of Rick's decorated sugar cookies.

"I knew it," Jamie said once the door shut behind the customer. "They're wiping out all of the stores."

She placed the iPad on the sales counter and turned it so Lucy could get a proper view of the architectural plans.

Lucy swept crumbs from the countertop and glanced at the tablet.

"Just like Tanner Falls," Jamie said for added emphasis.

"Really?" Lucy pulled a face.

"Yep. And Sawyer is a part of it." A *big* part. Huge. As in, he was the literal architect of her worst nightmare. "I cannot believe he didn't tell me."

Lucy tilted her head, thinly veiled amusement dancing in her eyes. "How long did you two date?"

Jamie wasn't entirely sure how to answer that question. Until he'd broken up with her and left Waterford, it seemed as if Sawyer had always been a part of her life. "Well, we met in the eighth grade but didn't start dating until our sophomore year."

Lucy's gaze narrowed. "Were you Prom Queen and King?"

"He was king." Sawyer had always been the popular one. Jamie, not so much. "I was the girl who stayed late in the library, focusing on my books and studies."

Lucy laughed. "Of course you were."

"Yeah, you would think those differences would've driven us apart, especially being so young. But..." Her heart gave a bittersweet tug. "That wasn't until after graduation."

"What happened?"

Jamie took a deep breath. "Well, right before he left for college, he came to me to give me this big speech about how we were way too young to be so serious, especially with him going off to Columbia and me staying here at Reed. You know, we had our 'whole futures to consider.' We broke up. And that was that."

That *wasn't* that. Not exactly. She'd not-so-casually left out the part about being a heartbroken mess for the whole summer after that painful conversation.

Sawyer had been the love of her life back then. In the years since, she'd never come close to loving someone that way. Not Matt, not anyone. Sometimes she thought Sawyer O'Dell was *still* the love of her life.

Not anymore, though. Not since he'd decided to shut down her bookstore.

"I'm sorry, honey." Lucy reached for Jamie's hand, gave it a gentle squeeze, and then released it.

"Oh, it was a long time ago." Jamie shrugged. But an ache formed in her throat, and she didn't quite trust herself to keep talking about Sawyer and her broken schoolgirl heart without doing something silly and pointless like dissolving into tears. So she pointed at the new cookies Rick had recently dropped off—Scottish shortbread, shaped like hearts and covered with dark choco-late drizzle. "Have you tried these, by the way? They are *amazing*."

Lucy gathered a stack of books lying by the register and headed to the sales area to re-shelve them. "Rick's working on a new recipe."

"Ohhh..." Jamie loved it when Rick ex-perimented, especially when his efforts involved chocolate.

"Oh, that reminds me. You're coming with me tonight." Lucy swerved deftly around a woman in a dark blue raincoat whose head was buried deep in one of the newly released romance novels.

Jamie had no choice but to follow. "Where?"

"Rick's Valentine cooking class." Lucy held up a finger. "And no 'I'm writing' excuses. I need you there in case I meet someone. That way we can discuss the pros and cons."

Ahh, just the opening she needed. "And what about Rick?"

You're welcome, Rick.

"Yeah." Lucy shrugged. "I'll ask Rick's opinion, too. You know, guy's perspective. But first, I need to meet my own true love."

Seriously? How could she be so clueless? Rick had practically been tossing rose petals in her path every time he saw her and somehow Lucy still hadn't realized he was madly in love with her.

Jamie sighed. "Well, how do you know you haven't already met him? I mean, Waterford isn't exactly Portland in terms of population."

Lucy shook her head. "Oh, no. I will know when I meet him. We will *both* have that moment where we just...know." She cocked her head, dreamy-eyed. "You know?"

Then she frowned down at the book in her hands. "Wait. This goes someplace else."

Lucy bustled to the other side of the shop, leaving Jamie to ponder the existence of such a magical moment.

What had she said, exactly?

Jamie gnawed on her bottom lip.

We will both *have that moment when we just... know. You know?*

"Hmm. No, I don't know." Jamie had never experienced such a moment. Sure, she'd read about them, but she'd never once had one herself. And she wouldn't *be* having one anytime soon, if ever, because she was still very much on a dating hiatus. Nothing had changed in that department, and it wouldn't.

Especially not while Sawyer was back in town.

Sawyer juggled his messenger bag in one hand and a small shopping basket in the other as he followed Rick up and down the aisles of Aubergine Specialty Foods in the business district. Somehow, when he'd asked Sawyer to be his wingman for his Valentine cooking class, he'd left out the part about shopping for groceries.

Aubergine was the sort of grocery store where only someone like Rick would shop. A true foodie's paradise. For starters, it was minuscule, crammed full of tiny twenty-dollar bottles of olive oil, pasta imported from Italy and gourmet cheeses Sawyer had never heard of. It also had a crisp black-and-white striped awning out front and a sidewalk fruit stand, as if someone had plucked it right off the streets of Europe and dropped it in Waterford. The fancy little shop definitely hadn't been around back when Sawyer was in high school.

Plenty of things had changed since then. Sawyer knew this. He was just having kind of a hard time adjusting to Waterford's new reality.

"Why didn't you tell me that Jamie bought

True Love Books?" he said to the back of Rick's head while his friend perused the selection of spices.

Rick grabbed a small bottle of peppercorns and placed it carefully in the basket. "Remember a few years ago when I casually mentioned she was dating that dentist? Your reaction was to tell me to never let you know anything about Jamie because it distracted you."

Distracted. That was one word for it. A more accurate description probably would have been that thinking about Jamie with another man made him crazy.

Sawyer cleared his throat. "Vaguely."

"Well, you did." Rick shrugged and added something else to the shopping basket. "So I didn't."

"Anything else you're not telling me?" he asked, doing his best to ignore the sudden throbbing in his temples. He'd known coming back to Waterford to help secure the Ridley project might get complicated, but this was beyond complicated. This was a disaster in the making.

"She's not happy about the project," Rick said nonchalantly.

Sawyer's jaw clenched. He wondered if Aubergine carried ibuprofen. Doubtful. "Yeah, I get that already."

"And she's single." Rick shot him a smile and rounded the corner toward the produce section.

Sawyer paused. So Jamie Vaughn was single?

Now this was the sort of pertinent information he was most interested in.

Not that it mattered. Whatever he and Jamie once shared had been over for a long time. Fifteen years, as she'd been so quick to remind him.

He chased Rick down and found him contemplating a purple cluster of radicchio. "So what happened with the dentist?"

Rick abandoned the radicchio in favor of something that looked sort of like grass clippings. "He moved to Texas last year."

Sawyer let out a breath. "So they weren't that serious."

"Oh, no. They were serious." Rick picked up another bundle of weeds, smelled them and added them to his pile. "But he got some job offer that he couldn't turn down. He asked her to move with him. She declined."

"Why?" Sawyer's throat grew tight.

He couldn't help comparing himself and the mystery dentist who had asked her to move with him across the country. It was more than Sawyer had done when he'd left for Columbia.

But they'd been kids. It would've been crazy to make such a serious commitment at that age. Right?

He found it more and more difficult to swallow while he waited for Rick to respond.

"You'll have to ask her," he finally said.

Sure, because that would go over really well. Jamie probably couldn't wait to have a good old-fashioned heart-to-heart with the man who wanted to tear down her precious bookstore and put something "hideous" in its place.

"Given how she reacted when she found out I was working with Ridley, that feels highly unlikely."

He couldn't even blame her. The plans for the new development definitely didn't include keeping True Love in its present form. But how could he have known the bookstore belonged to her now?

Her words from their walk in the courtyard spun round in his mind, taunting him.

I bought it a few years ago, just like I always said I would.

Maybe he *should* have known. Once Jamie made up her mind to do something, she usually made it happen.

"Does she date anyone now?" he asked, dreading the answer. Rick had said she was single, but Sawyer had a hard time believing it.

"No one." Rick tossed a lemon in the air, caught it and shrugged. "She's on a 'romantic hiatus.'"

Sawyer laughed. "That does sound like something she would say."

"Lucy thinks that, instead of dating, Jamie pours all her heart into the bookstore." Rick gave him a grim smile. "The very one that you're trying to tear down."

Yeah. Thanks for the reminder.

Rick slapped him on the back, but it was hardly reassuring.

It's not like that, he started to say. But then he stopped and sighed. The throbbing in his temples grew worse, until the ache was almost unbearable.

It was exactly like that.

With hours to go until closing time and not an inkling of a plan to save the store, Jamie passed the afternoon by dusting. *Aggressively* dusting, if such a thing were possible. Her feather duster flew across book spines in a furious effort to not only clean, but somehow whip up an idea—*any* idea—to push back against Ridley.

Which obviously meant pushing back against Sawyer too. They shared a history together, but that didn't mean she was going to play nice. She couldn't *afford* to play nice. Her entire livelihood was at stake, plus decades of True Love history as a Waterford landmark.

"We have to find a way to fight back," she announced as she ran the feather duster over the top of the pink and gold piano in the *Poetry* corner.

Lucy shoved a copy of *The Love Letters of John Keats* into place on its shelf. "Okay, but how?"

"I have exactly no idea. But we have got to

come up with something." Jamie stabbed at the air with her feather duster. "I mean, this place just means too much for them to cavalierly tear it down."

She picked up a little wooden duck knick-knack to clean beneath it, despite zero evidence of dust bunnies. Come to think of it, she might have already dusted the entire piano an hour ago. Ugh. She placed the duck back in front of the row of poetry books lined up on the piano's lid, but her knuckles knocked into a wax embosser kit in the process. She reached for the knob of the wax seal stamp, but it toppled off the piano quicker than she could catch it, slipping into the narrow space between the instrument and the wall.

"Oops." Crouching down while wearing a pencil skirt was never ideal, but Jamie managed. Her hand slid into the tiny crack, but as she reached for the stamp, her fingertips came into contact with something bigger and bulkier.

She squinted into the dark space and caught sight of whatever it was, then slid her arm as far as it would go to grab hold of it. Success! She pulled it forward, and out tumbled the wax seal stamp along with a pale pink volume with *The Story of Us* printed on the cover in swirling gold script.

"What is that?" Lucy said as Jamie straightened.

"It's a book." Jamie had never heard of it, though. She'd definitely never seen it in the store before, so she flipped it open to take a peek. But as the cover lifted, she realized it wasn't a book at all. It was a box designed to resemble a book, and it was filled with colorful cards decorated with hearts and flowers, yellowed with age.

She gasped. "It's *not* a book. These are Valentines!"

Lucy peered over her shoulder, chose one of the cards from the box and opened it. "These are so cute."

Jamie sifted through the Valentines. There must have been forty or fifty of them, at least. Most featured retro illustrations—a watercolor of a puppy carrying an envelope sealed with a heart, a tiny elfin girl eating candy from a frilly heart-shaped box. They were the sort of Valentines that pre-dated the cartoon cards children passed out at school nowadays. These were special. Precious...

But what were they doing tucked away in a box in a corner of her store?

She scanned the writing inside one of the cards and gasped. "These are Valentines from old True Love customers to True Love Books."

"Awww." Lucy pressed a Valentine to her heart. "This is ridiculously sweet."

Lucy grabbed a stack from the box and carried it to the white Queen Anne sofa in the reading nook by the front window. "Ah, look! This one says it's from 1965!"

Jamie lowered herself onto the sofa cushion beside her. "Mr. Ogilvy must have kept them."

"'Dear True Love,'" Lucy read. "'Without you we wouldn't have had our first Valentine's Day coffee and found our own true loves. You'll always have a place in our hearts. Love, Chris and Tara.'"

For the first time all day, Jamie's sagging spirits lifted. She chose another card to read aloud. "'A Valentine of appreciation to True Love Books & Cafe. You brought us together in the *classics* and helped us find our happily ever after. Forever grateful, Sam and Laurie.'"

Goosebumps cascaded over Jamie, head to toe. She'd always appreciated how important True Love was to Waterford, but she'd never seen such an outpouring of support for the store before. It was just what she needed, today of all days.

"We should put these out for the customers." Lucy began lining the Valentines up on the coffee table in a neat row.

"Yes! And show how important True Love is to the community!" Jamie's heart thumped as she was hit with a small epiphany. Her head snapped toward Lucy. "That's it!"

A few nearby customers glanced over in curiosity.

"What's it?" Lucy gave her blank stare.

Didn't she see? This was the answer Jamie had been trying so hard to come up with all day.

This box and its precious contents were exactly what she needed in order to prove that True Love was far more important than the awful industrial development that Ridley—and *Sawyer*—wanted to put in its place. These Valentines could be the very thing that saved her store.

"That's how we fight back!"

Chapter Six

*T*WO HOURS AND EIGHT PHONE calls later, Jamie finally managed to track down the Editor-in-Chief of the *Waterford Chronicle*. It wasn't easy. She'd had to navigate her way through a complicated phone tree of various voice mail messages, assistants and department editors, all while waiting on customers, closing up shop for the night and changing into appropriate evening attire for Rick's Valentine's cooking class. But all the effort was worth it, because the top dog himself finally took her call just as she and Lucy approached the door to Rick's Bistro & Trattoria.

She talked as quickly as she could, lest he grow bored with her story and end the call. Plus, Rick's class was supposed to have started five minutes ago.

"Yes. Yes, that's right—Valentine's cards from old True Love customers, people who met there. Some of them date back to the middle of last century!" Jamie paused on the threshold of the bistro just long enough to take a breath and let Lucy open the door for her. Technically, she could have opened it herself, but one hand was holding her iPhone while the other was gesticulating wildly. If she'd been wearing a Fitbit, smoke would have probably been coming out of it.

The editor took advantage of her need for oxygen to ask about the rumor he'd heard that True Love was a popular Waterford hotspot for couples to get engaged.

Jamie beamed at Lucy as she answered in the affirmative. It was actually happening! The newspaper was going to run a feature on True Love Books. She could feel it. "And yeah, this year alone we've had four proposals *in the store.*"

Lucy opened the second door—the one that led from the entry foyer to the main dining room of Rick's restaurant—and Jamie practically danced her way through it.

"Now isn't that a legacy worth saving?" she asked, really driving the point home.

Please let him agree. Please.

She bit her bottom lip while she waited for the editor to respond, feeling about as nervous as Eliot on bath day. When he said yes, she jumped up and down right there by the hostess stand in Rick's fancy bistro. She couldn't help it. Things were *finally* looking up.

"And when is it going to run?" She held her

breath and nearly fainted when she heard the word *tomorrow*. "Great! Thank you so much."

She jabbed the off button on her phone and squealed at Lucy, "We're in!"

Lucy held her hand up and they high-fived as if they'd just won gold at the Olympics. Honestly, it felt like they had. Tomorrow could be the turning point...by the end of the week, Sawyer might just pack up his hideous spaceship model and go crawling back to Portland. She wouldn't have to see him for another fifteen years.

If ever.

But as soon as she and Lucy finished their impromptu victory celebration, Jamie became aware of a loaded silence surrounding her. She glanced up, and sure enough, there was Sawyer O'Dell, leaning against Rick's polished mahogany bar, looking straight at her as he sipped a glass of red wine.

To add insult to injury, Aunt Anita stood right beside him, wine glass in hand. By all appearances, it looked like they were having quite a nice time together.

Naturally.

Anita didn't have a mean or judgmental bone in her body. She probably thought Sawyer was just doing his job.

Which he was. But that didn't mean Jamie had to like it. Also, she might have been more inclined to overlook his participation in the Ridley project if he'd been upfront and honest about why he was back in Waterford when they'd first crossed paths. He hadn't, though.

Not one little bit.

She greeted him with an exaggerated eye roll, the sum total of the politeness she felt he deserved. "Of *course* you're here."

Sawyer's lips tugged into an annoyingly charming half-grin. His gaze slid to Anita. "This *is* a small town."

Too small, actually—especially now.

Finally, something she and Sawyer could agree on.

Sawyer probably shouldn't have felt so smug about the shocked look on Jamie's face when she first spotted him at the bar, but he couldn't quite help it. He'd been surprised at every turn since arriving in Waterford, and now the shoe was back on the other foot.

Anita had filled him in over a nice glass of Sangiovese, so he'd known Jamie would be in attendance. From their discussion, he'd also managed to discern that Lucy was, in addition to being the object of Rick's affection, Jamie's employee and best friend. Rick, being Rick, had left out this crucial bit of intel when he'd recruited Sawyer into being his wingman. He'd definitely taken Sawyer at his word when he'd told him he no longer wanted to hear about Jamie.

That wasn't the case anymore, obviously. Now Sawyer wanted to know *everything*.

Purely for business purposes, of course. Still, his pulse kicked up a notch when Jamie slipped out of her red coat and he caught his first glimpse of her black chiffon dress with its sheer sleeves and flippy little skirt. He'd barely had a chance to get used to her librarian-chic polka-dotted pencil skirts, and now this. He was in no way prepared for the sight of grown-up Jamie Vaughn in a little black dress, the sudden hostility between them notwithstanding.

He somehow managed to look away, only to find that an amused Rick had been watching him watch Jamie. Sawyer sighed, and Rick's grin spread wide.

Fine. Maybe Rick's delight in Sawyer's current predicament would help him relax long enough to tell Lucy that he'd orchestrated this entire evening just for her. Sawyer certainly hoped so.

"Okay, everybody." Rick clapped his hands, and all eyes—including Lucy's—swiveled in his direction. In his crisp chef's whites, Rick looked like he'd just walked off the set of some show on the Food Network. With any luck, Lucy was into that sort of thing. "If you all would find a cooking station..."

Sawyer glanced at Jamie. This was, after all, a Valentine's event, and Rick had set up the cooking stations in pairs. Maybe in between all the dicing, chopping and sautéing, they could bury the hatchet—preferably not in each other.

Before he could suggest a truce, though, someone from the other side of the room called Jamie's name.

"Jamie?" Eric, the esteemed city councilman, grinned at her and pointed to a table near the front. "Would you like to..."

She lit up like a Christmas tree. "Yes, I would."

Sawyer's gut clenched as Jamie floated toward Eric, diaphanous black chiffon swirling around her legs. He told himself the only reason she seemed so excited about being Eric's partner was because he was on the town council. He also told himself that was the only reason it bothered him—the idea that she might gain another ally against his project. But coming up with a justification for that sinking feeling in his stomach was little consolation. He wasn't even sure he believed his excuses.

He turned toward Anita and offered her his elbow. "Well?"

"Okay. Thank you." She slipped her arm through his.

"All right." Sawyer nodded, and they made their way toward the cooking stations.

He absolutely did *not* choose the table next to Jamie and Eric's on purpose. It was simply where they landed...

Just in time to hear Eric tell Jamie how great she looked.

Jamie smiled up at him. "Thank you. You do too."

Sawyer had the sudden urge to stab a certain city councilman with the butter knife at his station. What. Was. Happening? There was a quiet storm brewing inside him, completely out of the blue. If he hadn't known better, he would have thought it was jealousy.

Fortunately—or not so fortunately for Rick—another disaster in the making tore Sawyer's attention away from Jamie's impromptu date and his own inconvenient sense of unease. Lucy appeared as if she was on the verge of pairing off with a stranger as her cooking partner, and that definitely wasn't part of the plan. An unattached guy in a chunky cardigan was smiling and crossing the room toward her with determined footsteps.

Oh, boy.

Rick cast a panicked glance at Sawyer. What was he supposed to do—physically throw himself between them? That seemed extreme, even for a wingman.

"Hi." Lucy returned Sweater Guy's smile. "Do you want to…"

She pointed at the only unoccupied cooking station, and Sweater Guy nodded. "Sure."

"I'm Lucy." Lucy extended her hand.

Sweater Guy shook it gently, and then offered

her one of the aprons from their station. "I'm Quinten."

Lucy pulled the apron over her head. "I like your sweater."

Ouch.

At the head of the class, Rick visibly wilted, his spirit sinking faster than a ruined soufflé. Sawyer needed to do something. Fast.

He cleared his throat as he tied his own apron in place. "All right, Chef. What is on the menu?"

It worked—temporarily, at least. The room grew quiet as the attendees waited to hear what they would be cooking.

"We're going to start off with an arugula salad, marinated figs, cherry tomatoes and feta cheese." Rick sighed, shoulders slumped.

"Mmmm," Lucy said, loud enough for everyone—including Rick—to hear.

Rick brightened somewhat. "Followed by our entree of miso-glazed salmon, roasted potatoes and bok choy."

Lucy gasped. "I love glazed salmon!"

Shocker.

Sawyer bit back a smile. Watching Rick attempt to woo a woman by way of seafood would've been painful if it weren't so amusing. He'd never seen Rick so off his game before.

"What's for dessert?" Sawyer prompted, because again, Rick couldn't seem to do more than just stand there staring at Lucy with a panicked grin plastered on his face.

"Raspberry chocolate torte."

Nice choice. The room erupted into *oohs* and *ahhs*.

Rick managed to take a breath and laugh until Lucy gave Sweater Guy a playful punch as she shouted, "Yes!"

Sawyer figured he was in for a long night. He wasn't sure if anyone had ever needed to wingman this hard in the entire history of wingmaning. He met Rick's gaze, nodded and did a little shadow boxing motion.

Don't give up, champ.

His attempt at subtle encouragement didn't go unnoticed—not by Jamie, anyway. When Sawyer glanced over at her, he found her glowering at him, mouth agape.

His face went warm. "What?"

While Rick answered questions from a few of the attendees, Jamie murmured to Sawyer, "Oh, I mean, I just think if a guy wants to say something to a woman—like 'Hey, I like you' or 'Hey, I'm actively employed by the company trying to tear down your store'—that *direct* communication goes a lot further than dancing around the topic or, you know, being vague about it." She wagged a finger back and forth between Sawyer and Rick. "But you guys do you."

Sawyer shifted uncomfortably from one foot to the other. Beside him, Anita shook with silent laughter. Councilman Eric just seemed confused, and Sawyer was in no mood to fill him in.

"Okay, if one partner would head to the back and grab some salad fixings..." Rick pointed at a long table set up behind the cooking stations.

Jamie—clearly energized by her wave of indignation—grabbed a silver bowl and a pair of tongs and took off as if she'd been shot out of a cannon.

Sawyer followed, hot on her heels. "I'm sorry I didn't mention my involvement with Ridley when I first saw you at the bookshop."

There. He'd said it. He'd apologized.

She whipped around to face him, blond ringlets flying. Her skin was so beautiful, it made Sawyer want to weep. "Thank you."

"But, in my defense..." He just couldn't keep his mouth shut because, after all, he wasn't totally in the wrong. "I didn't know it was *your* bookshop until just then."

"But you knew it was True Love and you knew how much that place means to me." She grabbed a chunk of arugula with her tongs.

Was she seriously not going to cut him the tiniest bit of slack? He was just doing his job. He shook his head and shoveled arugula into his bowl. "Well, yeah, but not for a long time."

"No, it wasn't a long time ago to me. And if you think your being a part of Team Ridley is going to stop me from saving True Love, then you have another thing coming." She clicked her tongs together right in his face for emphasis. The effect was surprisingly ominous.

Sawyer grabbed his bowl and chased after

her. He still knew Jamie well enough to know when she was up to something. The high fives when she'd walked in with Lucy, the wielding of kitchen implements...these things weren't insignificant.

"What are you cooking up?" he asked once they'd returned to their side-by-side cooking stations.

She blinked at him with exaggerated innocence. "Miso-glazed salmon. Weren't you paying attention?"

"I was paying attention." In fact, he'd been paying Jamie Vaughn far more attention than he wanted to admit. "And *you* are planning something."

She completely ignored him, focusing instead on the food at her table and Eric, whose presence was really turning out to be a thorn in Sawyer's side for reasons he didn't want to contemplate.

"Sawyer?" Rick said.

"What?" he snapped.

Rick aimed a quizzical look at the bowl in Sawyer's hands and motioned toward the cluster of his classmates lingering by the table of ingredients. "Do you want to give everybody else some arugula?"

What the...?

Sawyer glanced down. "Oh."

His bowl overfloweth. Arugula spilled over the rim and onto the floor. He'd been so distracted that he hadn't left a single leaf behind for the other cooking students.

Titters of laughter broke out, and when Sawyer looked back up, every pair of eyes in the room was on him—with the notable exception of Jamie and Eric, who only seemed to have eyes for each other.

The night was getting longer by the second. He winced. "Sorry."

Was it time for dessert yet?

Chapter Seven

To Jamie's immense delight, the *Waterford Chronicle* article about True Love Books & Cafe was splashed across the front page of the Arts & Culture section the following morning. A photograph she'd sent the editor was printed alongside it—Jamie, standing by the bookstore's front counter and holding up the box of Valentines she'd found behind the piano.

The response to the story was overwhelmingly supportive, beyond anything Jamie could have possibly imagined. To her complete and utter astonishment, the story went viral shortly before noon, with enough tweets, retweets and Facebook posts to spread news of the impending threat to her bookshop far and wide.

Customers poured in, not just from Waterford, but from the surrounding towns as well. They lingered by the cherry tree display at the front of the store where Jamie and Lucy had strung up the old Valentine cards from The Story of Us box, securing them with glittery gold ribbon and pink clothespins. Some customers stayed for hours, reading each and every handwritten message while sipping coffee or nibbling one of Rick's heart-shaped cookies. They bought books, too! Love stories by the armful. Jamie darted back and forth between the storeroom and the sales floor, trying to keep up with the demand. Meanwhile, the cupcake supply dwindled at an alarming rate. By two o'clock, she was forced to make an emergency run to Rick's Bistro to pick up more.

She took advantage of her time away to make a quick stop at Anita's Flowers to share the exciting news with her aunt. The store had been so busy that Jamie hadn't had a spare second to talk to her about the article, much less the sudden boom in business. Her fingertips flew over her tablet, opening the newspaper's webpage. She practically shoved it at Aunt Anita the minute she stepped inside her shop.

Anita insisted on reading the article aloud, even though Jamie had practically memorized every word of it.

"'Is romance on your mind? True Love Books & Cafe in Waterford may be the place to go. With dozens of proposals and successful first dates in its history, some say the bookstore and café is love's lucky charm. While we'll never know for sure, many former customers believe in its romantic magic so much, they've been sending thank-you Valentines to the store for decades.'" Anita paused for a breath before getting to the last line, Jamie's favorite part. "'Isn't this just the type of Waterford legacy worth saving?'"

Jamie liked those words more and more every time she heard them. She'd actually done it! She'd managed to completely change the narrative surrounding the proposed Ridley development. No one in town was talking about Sawyer's fancy plans anymore. Now they were talking about things that actually mattered—things like True Love Books and romance and community.

"Oh, this is wonderful, Jamie." Anita looked up, grinning from ear to ear. "Was the article your idea?"

Jamie nodded and hugged the tablet to her chest when Anita returned it to her, then followed her aunt to a display cooler filled with long-stemmed roses. "I did the interview yesterday. I probably should've thought of it before, but it didn't occur to me until I found the Valentines and with the vote coming up—which, did you hear?"

Anita shook her head as she pulled the cooler door open. "No."

"It got moved up," Jamie said. The town council had announced the new date less than an hour ago. "To February fourteenth."

"Valentine's Day?" Anita plucked a few white roses from a vase and frowned. "So soon?"

"I guess Ridley is putting pressure on them to make a decision." Jamie was convinced the sudden interest in True Love was behind the abrupt schedule change. "But honestly, this article has generated so much interest in the store. We have people coming in from Portland. And Eugene! Lucy called this morning and said there was a line already outside the door."

Jamie couldn't believe it. The last time she'd seen anyone form a line outside a store anyplace in Oregon was at the popular donut shop in Portland—the one with the pink boxes and all those crazy donut flavors. This kind of excitement and enthusiasm for her shop felt like a miracle.

"Will it be enough, though?" Anita chose two more white roses and closed the cooler door.

Jamie followed her to the counter where a floral arrangement sat waiting, half-assembled. "What do you mean?"

"If you stop Ridley Properties this time, won't a development team just come right in behind them?" Anita placed the flowers on the counter and peered at Jamie over the top of her glasses. Something about the look in her eyes dampened Jamie's glee over True Love's sudden popularity. "I mean, it sure seems like the council has their sights set on wiping this whole area clean and starting over."

No, that couldn't be true. Jamie refused to believe it. "Actually, it's pretty evenly split. Which means that Eric will have the final say, and he's very open to listening."

He'd been so attentive at the cooking class. Granted, she hadn't had much of a chance to talk to him about the Ridley situation since Sawyer had been within earshot for practically the entire night.

Anita smirked. "Or he notices a pretty woman is the face of the opposition."

"It's not like that," Jamie corrected. There was no room for anyone named Eric in a romantic hiatus. Zero.

Anita shook her head and laughed. "Oh, honey. I saw how he looked at you at the cooking class. Sawyer saw it, too."

She shot an amused glance at Jamie and then strolled toward the other side of the flower shop, forcing Jamie to scurry after her.

"Sawyer?" Jamie cleared her throat, lest she sound overly interested in anything he might think. "What did Sawyer say?"

"He didn't say anything." Anita paused at a shelf full of colorful glass vases and chose a frosted green one for her arrangement. "I mean, after your little spat..."

"It was not a spat." Jamie rolled her eyes so hard it was almost painful. "*Couples* have spats. We had a...vigorous disagreement."

"However you want to put it." Anita waved a dismissive hand. "The point is, Sawyer kept watching both of you through the whole class."

Why did this inconvenient nugget of information send a little thrill skittering through Jamie's veins? And why did she suddenly have to bite down hard on her bottom lip to stop herself from smiling?

She squared her shoulders and reminded herself how much she was starting to loathe Sawyer O'Dell and his hideously modern architectural aesthetic. "Well, there's nothing going on between me and Eric. Especially after..."

Anita arched a single, accusatory eyebrow. "Sawyer?"

Seriously? She hadn't dated the man in over a decade. She'd moved on...mostly. "Matt! The guy I was just dating who moved away?"

"But to be fair to Matt, he wanted you to go with him," Anita said.

"Unlike Sawyer, who just left."

Anita tilted her head. "To go to *college*."

"Whose side are you on?" Jamie said, only half-seriously. She knew good and well that Anita had always been her biggest supporter.

"Always yours." Anita laughed, then pointed to Jamie's tablet. "Which is why I'm so proud of you for that."

"Thank you." A fresh wave of happiness coursed through her—as it should. There was absolutely no reason why Jamie should spoil her triumphant day by thinking about Sawyer. Or their long-ago breakup. Or her heart's annoying habit of skipping a beat every time she ran into him.

Jamie's gaze flitted over her aunt's shoulder toward a cluster of bobbing red balloons with the word *Love* printed on them in shiny silver letters. She wondered briefly if anyone made balloons that said *Romantic Hiatus*.

Probably not.

"I wonder what the feedback will be like from the Ridley side?" Anita began tucking her new arrangement into the vase. White roses and baby's breath spilled over the edge, perfectly offset by deep emerald leaves.

She's so good at this, Jamie thought. The flower shop was just as important to the community as True Love Books & Cafe—maybe even more so. Anita had seen just about everyone in town through the myriad of life's ups and downs—weddings, birthdays, funerals. Waterford needed Anita's Flowers.

Jamie shrugged in answer to her aunt's question but hope fluttered deep in her belly. With any luck, the feedback from Ridley would be a big white flag of surrender. Then everything could go back to the way it had been before. No more Ridley. No more scary fliers from the town council.

No more Sawyer O'Dell.

Sawyer knew something had gone terribly wrong when he was awakened by a text from Dana before the sun came up.

He squinted at his phone in the semi-darkness of Rick's spare bedroom, wondering what could have possibly happened overnight to warrant the dressing down that seemed to be coming his way. Dana's words were brief and to the point.

Get to the office in Portland immediately.

He suddenly felt like he was right back at Waterford High, being summoned to the principal's office, especially when Dana's initial text was followed quickly by another, more dauntingly specific message.

We need to discuss Jamie Vaughn.

Something inside Sawyer's chest closed into a tight fist. He *knew* Jamie was up to something. She'd acted far too smug for his liking last night at Rick's Valentine's class. He'd done his best to keep things as civil as possible. He'd even extended an olive branch and apologized. But Jamie hadn't cut him any slack whatsoever. She'd just waxed poetic about her precious bookstore and batted her eyelashes at Eric over their plate of mediocre salmon. Rick's professional-grade recipe had been a tough nut to crack.

Except Jamie hadn't technically been batting her lashes or flirting in any obvious way. Still, Sawyer's throat had grown thick every time she'd laughed at something Eric said or simply looked at her cooking partner with anything other than the veiled disgust she reserved specifically for Sawyer these days. And their salmon hadn't looked anywhere near as mediocre as what he and Anita had managed to cook up. Everything Jamie and Eric whipped up looked nearly identical to Rick's sample plate. Rick had even bragged about what a "great team" they made.

He found it nauseating…in a completely neutral, non-jealous sort of way, of course.

Sawyer shook his head.

You are losing it, my friend.

The arugula didn't lie.

At least he didn't have it as bad as Rick—genuinely interested in a relationship with Lucy, who'd also spend the entire evening alongside another man, despite all wingman-ing efforts to the contrary. It wasn't as if Sawyer was seriously looking to rekindle anything with Jamie. He was just confused, or caught up in some aching whirlwind of nostalgia, taunted by the age-old question of what might have been. The pull he felt every time she walked into the room wasn't anything significant.

It couldn't be.

In any case, that magnetic pull certainly didn't work both ways. Jamie despised him. She'd made that perfectly clear. Maybe getting out of Waterford for a few hours was just what he needed to get his head back in the game.

He threw off the covers and got dressed within a matter of minutes, then quietly left the house so as not to disturb Rick. Once behind the wheel of his car, travel coffee mug in hand, he finally conducted a cursory search on his tablet for any Jamie-related news. It wouldn't hurt to know what he was in for once he got to the Ridley offices.

An article popped up immediately—a piece from the local Waterford paper that had been linked to by half a dozen regional news sites and every social media outlet he'd ever heard of. She'd gone viral.

Find Your True Love at True Love: Is romance on your mind? True Love Books & Cafe in Waterford may be the place to go.

Great.

Sawyer groaned within the confines of his Subaru. Now it looked as if Ridley—and by extension, Sawyer himself—wasn't only trying to close down a beloved bookstore but was also actively standing in the way of romance itself. No wonder Jamie and Lucy had been high-fiving all over the place last night. And no wonder Dana seemed so eager to take him to task.

He made it Portland in record time—less than three hours—eager to get the painful meeting over with. As he expected, Dana was ready and waiting for him in the sleek white conference room when he arrived. He pasted on a grin and strode inside.

Dana waved off his greeting and pointed to a silver mesh angular chair where he obediently took a seat. His backside barely had a chance to make contact with it before she handed him an iPad. He looked down, and Jamie's face smiled up at him from the photograph accompanying the now-famous article about True Love's importance to Waterford. He'd barely looked at the picture when he'd first pulled up the article earlier, more concerned with the contents of the story itself. Now, however, he couldn't seem to tear his gaze away from it.

Hair tumbling over her shoulders in loose blond curls, Jamie wore a soft gray sweater with pale pink stipes—cashmere, from the looks of it. Light spilled in from True Love's big picture window, casting a gentle glow over the box of Valentines in her hand and the shelves of books behind her, almost making the photograph look as if it had been taken in another era. Timeless. Beautiful.

Sawyer couldn't help being struck by the softness of the image and how much it contrasted with the room in which he now sat, all hard edges and glossy surfaces. The difference made him feel inexplicably hollow all of a sudden, so he forced his attention back to Dana looming over him less than a foot away.

She gave him a stiff smile. "Your goal was to persuade the community to embrace our deal."

"I know." He nodded, gaze flitting automatically back to the picture of Jamie.

The back of his neck grew warm.

Focus.

Dana took a deep, measured breath. "To be

very clear, this?" She pointed at the iPad—more specifically, to the headline that implied readers could find the love of their lives at True Love Books & Cafe. "Is the opposite of that."

"I understand." Sawyer handed her back the tablet. He couldn't concentrate with Jamie smiling up at him as if she were Cupid disguised as a beautiful bookseller. "Which is why I'm working to meet as many of the owners as possible."

He'd taken advantage of the drive from Portland to formulate a plan of action. Obviously, convincing Jamie to back the Ridley redesign was out of the question. Trying to get her on board would be next to impossible. But that didn't mean all of the other business owners in Waterford would follow her lead. He already had Rick on his side, and some of the people at the town council meeting had seemed interested, as well. What he needed to do was charm the socks off everyone else in the business district. Strength in numbers and all that.

"Well, perhaps you should concentrate on Ms. Vaughn," Dana said.

Sawyer stood. He'd had about enough of feeling like a chastened schoolboy. It was time to regain control of the situation. "Look, I know that Jamie can be a little passionate about her causes."

"Jamie?" Dana's eyebrows shot up. "How well do you know Ms. Vaughn?"

He cleared his throat. "Well, I haven't seen her since high school."

"But *in* high school?"

"We..." Sawyer paused. *We were as in love as two high school kids could be.* "...dated."

Dana blinked. "She was your high school sweetheart?"

This conversation was going even worse than Sawyer had imagined. He shook his head. "We never referred to ourselves..."

"Sawyer." Dana arched a perfectly shaped eyebrow.

He sighed. "Yes. We were high school sweethearts."

"And now?"

"We're nothing." But that wasn't the complete truth. Not the way Sawyer saw it, anyway. "A friendly nothing. We did just take a cooking class together last night."

Dana nodded. "That's good. Because there can be no lingering animosity between the two of you that could imperil this deal."

He thought back to last night—to Jamie's outburst about direct communication...to her salad tongs snapping together dangerously close to his face...

To the arugula.

"I've got it," he lied. "I've got it under control."

Chapter Eight

*T*HE AFTERNOON AT TRUE LOVE Books & Cafe proved to be even busier than the morning had been as more and more people had a chance to read the article and come by to support the bookshop. Jamie rang up books while Lucy tried her best to keep up with the coffee demand, which was *great*. Their espresso machine had never seen so much action.

Neither had True Love, obviously. The Valentine's display area was packed with well-dressed customers who seemed to be shopping for more than just books and lattes. Now that word had gotten out about the store being a lucky charm for love, Jamie noticed customers sneaking curious glances at one another and using the display of old Valentines as an ice breaker to meet each other. All in all, it was adorable.

And busy! So *very* busy.

When at last Jamie had a second to breathe,

she and Lucy met in the middle of the sales floor, halfway between the book register and the café counter, to do a tiny victory dance and marvel at what was happening around them.

"I just sent out an SOS to Rick," Lucy said. "We are almost out of sugar cookies!" Her face was flushed, and if Jamie wasn't mistaken, her black turtleneck smelled faintly of buttercream.

"Isn't this fantastic?" Jamie grinned, then crossed her arms. "That'll teach him."

"Who? Mr. Arugula?"

Of course. Who else? "Mm-hmm."

Sawyer should have known better than to try and get between her and True Love. She hated to think the article might cause him any real trouble with Ridley, but she hadn't had a choice. Honestly, he had no one to blame but himself. And why should she be worried about Sawyer's career when he clearly had no qualms about tearing down her store?

Lucy slid her sideways glance. Jamie got the impression she had some definite thoughts about Sawyer—traitor that he was—but before Lucy could voice them, Jamie's cell phone started vibrating in her hand.

She frowned down at it. "Oh."

"What?" Lucy said.

Jamie turned her iPhone toward Lucy so she could see the name lit up on the screen: *Matt.*

"Whoa. Matt?" Lucy's eyes grew wide. "What does your ex want?"

Jamie had no idea, but she suspected it might have something to do with his mom's recent surprise visit to True Love. Whatever the reason, she didn't have time to deal with it right now. What exactly was happening, anyway, with the recent parade of ex-boyfriends marching back through her life?

"And speaking of blasts from the past..." Lucy nudged Jamie with her elbow.

She looked up to see Sawyer standing on the opposite side of the room, all warm brown eyes and chiseled, masculine bone structure. He was wearing his Captain Wentworth peacoat again, *smiling* at her as if they were still on good terms... still a team, like they'd been all those years ago.

Sawyer + Jamie 4 ever. Those words had covered every inch of her favorite spiral notebook back in tenth grade. She hadn't thought about that notebook in years. Her heart gave a little flutter. Her stupid, stupid heart.

"Hmm." It was all she could manage to say. Why was he there? What could Sawyer possibly want with her now?

She pressed decline on her phone, silencing Matt's call.

"Yeah." Lucy shot her a meaningful glance and then scurried back to the café counter, leaving Jamie all alone, heart pounding as Sawyer strode toward her.

She felt like a deer in headlights all of a sudden, which was patently ridiculous. The tables had turned. True Love had the upper hand now, not Ridley. There was no reason she should feel so...so...breathless in Sawyer's presence.

It was beyond annoying, so she ignored it, squared her shoulders and marched in Sawyer's direction until they met one another mere inches from the Valentine display.

"Nice article," he said without an ounce of sarcasm. She barely took in the words, distracted as she was by the sight of his familiar, handsome face surrounded by the gold ribbons and vintage Valentines hanging overhead.

Somewhere at home, she still had a white bakery bag filled with all the Valentines that Sawyer had given her through the years—every single one. She should have thrown the bag away years ago, but she could never bring herself to get rid of it. Now, she wasn't quite sure whether that made her sentimental or pathetic.

Both, probably.

"Thanks," she said.

So this was it? He'd come by just to compliment her on her latest attempt to thwart his evil plan?

He leaned closer—close enough for her to get a whiff of cedar and woodsmoke from his peacoat, as if the lush, woodsy scents of Waterford still clung to him. The prodigal son. "But I have to ask—what did you think of my actual designs?"

She blinked. Surely he didn't want her actual, honest opinion.

"They're beautiful," she said after a beat. "And they will fit right in."

He grinned.

Not so fast. "In Sweden," she added.

Sawyer's brow furrowed as his smile died on his lips. "Sweden?"

"Yeah, like Nordic minimalism, which I'm actually a huge fan of myself." Who didn't love IKEA? Jamie was totally a fan of their meatballs. "It's just..."

"Just?" he prompted.

She shrugged. "Not Waterford."

Waterford was church bells and walks in the rain. It was flower boxes overflowing with blooms in the spring and piled high with snow in the winter. It was old brick buildings that lived and breathed history, not some impersonal sky-scraper without an ounce of meaning to the community.

She shouldn't have to explain this to Sawyer. He should *know*. He'd always known.

Then again, maybe he'd simply been away long enough to forget.

She cleared her throat. "Um, I should get back to work."

"Yeah." He nodded, clearly as ready as she was to end their conversation.

He'd seriously expected her to *compliment* his plans to run her out of business and turn their hometown upside down?

She waved a hand at their surroundings. If

he'd somehow forgotten where he'd come from, she was more than happy to remind him. "In my bookstore. Because..." She flashed him a self-satisfied smirk. "...it's busy."

His response was a frustrated grunt, and Jamie just walked away. Because really, there was nothing left to say. Besides, she had lattes to make, books to sell and a beloved Waterford institution to save.

From *him*.

If Sawyer had hoped stopping by True Love to talk to Jamie would somehow make him feel better, he'd been wrong. So very, very wrong.

He should have known better. Jamie had made her position crystal clear, which he'd tried to explain to Dana. But her comment about any "lingering animosity" he might have with Jamie had gotten under his skin. He didn't like to think there might be actual hard feelings between them. They were both simply doing their jobs, weren't they?

It's not personal. It's business.

He repeated these words to himself over and over again as he walked through the historic business district, back toward Rick's modern home. But no matter how many times he spun them around in his head, he still had a hollow feeling in the pit of his stomach. Probably because he knew there was no dividing line between personal and business matters where Jamie Vaughn was concerned. Jamie was hands-down, one hundred percent authentic and passionate about *everything* she did.

Sawyer had always loved her earnestness. It had been one of his favorite things about Jamie back in the day. But now...

Well, now it was driving him bonkers. And to make matters worse, it might just cost him his chance at a permanent place at Ridley.

"I have to do something to counter Jamie's article," he said, dropping onto one of the bar stools at the counter of Rick's sleek kitchen.

Rick glanced up from the pile of cremini mushrooms he was busy slicing into paper thin layers for salad. Sawyer hadn't anticipated being fed so many gourmet meals while in Waterford, but apparently that was a side benefit of staying with a chef. Definitely not terrible. "Good luck fighting against True Love."

"Have you been by there today? It's like a mosh pit."

"It's like every unattached person in town suddenly has an interest in the written word." Rick's chopping grew noticeably more aggressive. "Including *Quentin*."

Sawyer narrowed his gaze at his friend, who was now reaching for something in the huge sub-zero refrigerator built into his light oak kitchen cabinets. "Who's Quentin?"

"Sweater Guy from my cooking class." Hence the aggressive chopping. "Lucy and him exchanged phone numbers and now, according to Lucy—who likes to tell me these sorts of things—they're making plans for dinner."

He plopped a bowl of shiny red peppers onto the counter. "Which was not the outcome that I was going for."

"You know, Jamie had a point," Sawyer said, although he wasn't sure he should be pointing this out while Rick had a butcher knife in his hand. "You should tell Lucy how you feel."

"Yeah. Maybe I should've told her when she was a hundred percent single. But now she's not." Rick severed a pepper neatly in half with a single, purposeful slice.

"Whoa. They've only just talked." A conversation didn't mean anything. He would be willing to bet that he and Jamie had exchanged more words lately than Lucy and Sweater Guy. "She's still ninety-eight percent single."

Worst case scenario, ninety-five percent.

"Whatever. What about you and Jamie?" Rick said, as if he could see straight inside Sawyer's head.

Was he that obvious? "Wow, there was no effort at subtlety in that conversation pivot."

"Nope." Rick made quick work of chopping the peppers and added them to the bowl of sliced mushrooms and greens. "So? Have you talked to her since your cooking class disaster?"

Sawyer stood and paced a few feet, noticing

for the first time that Rick's kitchen sort of looked like an IKEA showroom, which of course reminded him of Jamie's comment about his designs for Ridley. What were her exact words, again?

Nordic minimalism.

Somehow, he didn't sense she'd meant them as a compliment.

"Briefly." He took a seat at the kitchen table and cast a forlorn look at his messenger bag, containing the plans he'd worked so hard on. "Meanwhile, only one store in the business district is willing to sit down with me. Olga's Dance Studio." Even the people who'd shown initial interest at the meeting were now making excuses about being too busy to talk.

Rick shrugged one shoulder. "That's the benefit of her having lived here longer than you. Jamie's in mostly everybody's ear."

"Yeah, but my sort-of being from Waterford is one of the reasons why Ridley gave me this shot. If they hire me, I won't have to travel so far for each project. And I might maybe eventually even be able to buy a house." An actual home, where he could chop his own vegetables and make his own fancy salad.

Okay, probably not. Between the two of them, Rick was the only gourmet chef. Realistically, Sawyer would probably still get take-out most nights, but it was a nice thought. Still, if he had his own house, he might at least invest in some decent cookware.

"You need to reintroduce yourself to folks, and

in a friendlier way," Rick said, abandoning the meal to join Sawyer at the table.

Thank goodness. He needed all the help he could get at the moment. He could eat once he had an inkling as to how he was going to save his career.

Maybe Rick was right, though. Perhaps all he needed to do was remind the good people of Waterford that he wasn't just some nameless, faceless stranger who worked for a development company intent on tearing everything down and rebuilding from scratch. He *cared* about Waterford. He was the same Sawyer O'Dell they'd once known and loved.

How could he show them that, though?

He bit the corner of his bottom lip and stared blankly at the spread of food on the bar—the crisp green salad, bowls of bright, colorful veggies and a fragrant, crusty loaf of homemade bread. His stomach growled, and his spirits lifted ever so slightly at the thought of a home cooked meal. Thank goodness Rick's restaurant was closed tonight.

Wait a minute. Wasn't there an old saying about the way to someone's heart being through their stomach?

"Embrace the community," he said, as inspiration struck.

Rick nodded slowly. "Embrace the community."

Jamie wasn't the only one who could charm socks off her neighbors. With a little luck—and a little help from the best chef in town—he could fight fire with fire.

Jamie burrowed into the cushions of her sofa and took a warm sip of strawberry rose herbal tea, exhausted from the busiest single sales day in True Love's long history. Gosh, if every day could be like this one, she wouldn't have to worry at all about going out of business. Nor would Aunt Anita or any of the other business owners, since more foot traffic in the district was good for everyone.

But she couldn't get ahead of herself. Right now, she simply needed take one day at a time while she battled Ridley. And Sawyer. Once the threat of a new development was no longer looming over her head, she could think about other ways to increase her bottom line. Today had been a raging success, by any standard. She deserved a few minutes of rest and relaxation with her favorite companion and the pitiful opening of her manuscript.

Eliot sat at her feet, meticulously licking his paw and rubbing it against his whiskers while a fire blazed in the hearth. Her laptop was *right there*, opened and waiting, but Jamie looked past it, toward *The Story of Us* box sitting on the coffee table.

She and Lucy had only managed to string up about half of the Valentines in the box so far. There were so many—it would take hours to read them all.

Meow. Eliot switched paws and went to work grooming his other whisker. Completely ignoring the blinking cursor on her computer screen, Jamie ran her hand over his soft ginger fur and then set her tea down on the coffee table. She dragged *The Story of Us* box into her lap and opened it.

She still couldn't believe it had been hidden in the store, right behind the pink piano, all this time. She wondered if Mr. Ogilvy had known about it, or if the Valentines had either fallen behind the piano or been deliberately placed there by the store's previous owners, a married couple who'd opened True Love Books back in 1945. She didn't know much about Harrison and Mary— just that Harrison sometimes went by Harris, and they'd built the bookshop from scratch and run it for decades until eventually retiring and leaving it to Mr. Ogilvy, a distant relative.

The whole thing was kind of mysterious. Mr. Ogilvy had always been something of a strong, silent type, parsing out bits and pieces of True Love's history to her little by little, over the many years she'd known him. The secrecy surrounding the bookstore only added to the appeal for Jamie, and made it more romantic, somehow.

She gathered a stack of Valentines from the box, wondering if one of them might help unravel the secrets of True Love's past. Then her gaze landed on a bundle of envelopes at the bottom of the box, tied together with a faded blue ribbon.

Even at first glance, she could see there was something different about these envelopes. They were thicker than the ones containing the Valentines, more discolored by age. Each one bore the same Waterford address, either in the upper left-hand corner or written larger in the space for the addressee. Jamie recognized all the other addresses as locations in Europe. The dates of the postmarks spanned three years, from 1941 to 1944.

Meow.

Eliot quit grooming himself to paw at the ribbon. Jamie could take a hint, so she untied it and handed it over. The kitty rolled onto his back and batted at the blue satin with his front feet while she opened the first letter.

Then a chill ran up her spine as she unfolded the yellowed paper and began to read.

> *Dearest,*
>
> *I know you told me not to write but you also told me to not wait for you while you go fight for our country. But you see, my darling, it is quite impossible for me to let you go. And so I will* wait for you and *give you glimpses of the world you have waiting for you here upon your return...*

Chapter Nine

*T*HE FOLLOWING DAY MARKED THE start of the set-up period for Waterford's upcoming Valentine's Day–themed Fire and Ice Festival, and since True Love had become far too busy to leave just one person in charge, Jamie and Lucy decided to close up shop for a little bit after the lunch rush to get a jump on things and move some supplies over to the festival grounds.

Was it easy to push a library cart loaded down with books and signage over bumpy, uneven cobblestones? No, definitely not. But Jamie made the best of it by telling Lucy all about the letters she'd discovered as they wheeled past the bookstore and headed toward the town square.

"They were so in love!" she gushed.

She couldn't stop thinking about all the intimate words she'd read the night before. She'd pored over the letters for hours with her breath caught in her throat, and by the time she'd got-

ten to the final one, tears had been streaming
down her face.

Lucy frowned. "Who?"

"Mary and Harris—the original owners of the
bookstore. I found some of their letters in The
Story of Us box. Harris broke up with Mary before
he was shipped overseas for World War II because
he didn't want her to wait for him." Sort of like
the way that Sawyer had broken up with Jamie
before he left Waterford for college, except their
story hadn't ended nearly as happily as Mary and
Harris's. "But she ignored him and kept writing
to him anyway."

What would've happened if she'd acted like
Mary and written to Sawyer after he'd moved
away? She couldn't shake the nagging question of
what if. At the time, she hadn't even considered
fighting for their future together. She'd simply accepted his decision and plunged headfirst into a
carton of ice cream. Wasn't that how heartbreak
was supposed to work?

But Harris had gone to *war.* He hadn't wanted
to tie Mary to him because he'd thought he might
die in battle and leave her heartbroken. Sawyer
had left to go to school, and she could only guess
he'd ended their relationship because he'd wanted to be free to chase after other girls. Really,
their situations had been completely different.
And if she and Sawyer had been soulmates—if
they'd been *destined* to be together, like Harris
and Mary—their breakup wouldn't have stuck.

Eventually, they would have found their way back to one another.

He is *back in town, remember?*

As if she could forget. Every time she turned around, Sawyer was right there...causing trouble for True Love at every turn.

"Good girl." Lucy nodded her approval of Mary's persistence.

"Yeah. Her letters about what was happening in Waterford were what kept him going while he was away." Sawyer, on the other hand, appeared not to care what had gone on in Waterford after he left. If he cared, he wouldn't be teaming up with Ridley Development to tear apart everything their town represented. If he cared, he would have come back to Waterford.

He would have come back to *her.*

A lump formed in her throat all of a sudden, which was ridiculous. Fifteen years had passed since she'd last shed a tear over Sawyer O'Dell, and she had no intention of doing so again.

She swallowed. Hard.

"Nowadays, she'd probably send him texts with some emojis mixed in." Lucy rolled her eyes as they slowed the library cart to a halt in the festival's assigned spot for True Love's booth.

The official kick off for the Fire and Ice Festival wasn't for another two days, but vendors had already begun setting up for the big Valentine's-themed celebration. As the business district's largest community event, it drew artisans and ice sculptors from all over the state.

"So not the same," Jamie said. An emoji-filled text versus a handwritten love letter? No contest.

Not that she'd been on the receiving end of either lately.

"It sounds romantic." Lucy sighed.

"Which makes sense for a couple who started a bookstore called True Love." Much to Jamie's annoyance, the lump in her throat seemed to double in size. "I mean, wouldn't that be nice? To have someone want to do something so creative with you like start a bookstore?"

Instead of tearing one down, which was the complete and total opposite.

Lucy looked her up and down. "I thought you were on a romantic hiatus."

Oh right. That.

"Doesn't mean I can't recognize romance in other people." Jamie squared her shoulders. She wasn't sure who she was trying to convince that she wasn't at all interested in having her own romance—Lucy or herself. Things had just gotten so confusing lately.

Luckily, before Lucy could ask more questions, a woman carrying two steaming cups approached them and offered one to each of them. Jamie wasn't sure what was inside, but it smelled chocolatey with a dash of cinnamon.

What a nice touch.

The festival had never handed out hot drinks

on set-up day before, but it was a lovely idea, especially on a brisk morning like this one.

Lucy accepted one of the cups with a smile. "Thank you."

Jamie did the same, the hot chocolate instantly warming her hands. But when her gaze landed on the blue geometric logo on the paper cup, she froze in place.

"Wait. What?" No...no, he did *not*. She turned the cup toward Lucy. "Does that say Ridley?"

What in the world? Had Sawyer signed Ridley up as a sponsor for the Fire and Ice Festival or something? She was sure that he'd never even *heard* of the festival until two days ago.

"Um. Don't look now, but..." Lucy's gaze darted to the opposite side of the town square and back again.

Jamie looked, because of course she did. Then she gasped out loud at what she saw. Not the most subtle of reactions, but she simply couldn't help it, because there stood Sawyer in front of a quaint, old-fashioned beverage cart, complete with a glossy, high-end espresso machine and huge sign that read *Free Coffee and Hot Chocolate, Courtesy of Ridley Property Development*.

And *of course* a small crowd had already gathered around his fancy cart, including several of the business district's shopkeepers—Chuck, from the pizzeria, and Beth, who owned a cute hobby shop just down the block from True Love Books.

Both of them chatted away with Sawyer while they sipped from Ridley cups.

Jamie didn't know whether to feel sick or enraged. Here she was, still smugly basking in the glow of yesterday's newspaper article, and meanwhile, Sawyer was apparently plying the good people of Waterford with cozy winter beverages in an effort to win them over to his side. It was beyond despicable.

And also kind of brilliant. She would have been impressed if she weren't too busy resenting him already.

Her grip tightened on her cup of evil hot chocolate. "No. Way."

Sawyer glanced over at her. Ugh, she'd actually said that out loud, hadn't she?

Yes, indeed. And the cocky little smile on his face left no doubt that he'd heard her, loud and clear.

He gave her a slight nod, then returned his attention to his coffee-swilling, hot chocolate-loving audience and said something that made them all throw their heads back and laugh.

Things had somehow just gone from bad to worse.

Sawyer would be lying if he'd said that the sight of Jamie Vaughn holding a cup with Ridley's logo didn't infuse him with a definitely sense of triumph. Maybe it was childish, but so be it.

Rick had been right. Embracing the community had been the way to go. His vintage barista stand had been attracting passersby for a solid two hours already, allowing him to engage in conversation with business owners from all over Waterford. It was amazing how willing they were to listen to what he had to say once they had complimentary caffeinated beverages in their hands. The cinnamon had been an especially deft touch—homey, just like Waterford itself. There wasn't an IKEA in the world that smelled like cinnamon.

"I love Waterford," he gushed, heady with victory. He was regaining some of the ground he'd lost in the wake of the viral article about True Love. He could feel it. "My mom and I moved here when I was twelve years old."

Sawyer then used the Ridley cup in his hand to motion toward Chuck, both for emphasis and to spread the comforting scents of cinnamon and chocolate far and wide. "Chuck, your dad gave me my first job at the pizzeria."

He'd been great at it. There'd been no arugula. And no Jamie Vaughn throwing a wrench in his plans at every turn.

"Oh, I remember." Chuck nodded. He looked exactly the same as he had back in high school—except for the thick beard. That was new.

"So, this isn't going to be just some random

teardown," he said, hoping they understood that he'd never let that happen. "I'm a hometown boy who's come back to his roots to do what I can to help make things better for a place I care a lot about."

It was the truth. He wasn't the big, bad monster Jamie seemed intent on making him out to be. He was on Waterford's side. The town council had reached out to Ridley for a proposal because they wanted a change—*needed* one in order to keep the business district going. This plan would be good for everyone. Sooner or later, she'd realize that.

Preferably sooner, because she'd already beat a hasty trail toward him from across the town square and was now staring at him with open skepticism.

"I'm sorry." She shook her head, as if what he'd just said made no sense whatsoever. "'*Hometown* boy?'"

He attempted a confident laugh, but it came out shakier than he'd planned. "That's me."

She arched a brow. "And when was the last time you were here?"

Jamie knew good and well how long he'd been away—fifteen years. In fact, she seemed to love throwing that number around as if it were confetti.

He flashed her a tight smile as Chuck and Beth looked on. "Um. Well. It's been...a while."

"Since you graduated high school," Jamie said flatly. "Right?"

The smiles on Chuck and Beth's faces faded ever so slightly. Was it only his imagination, or had they both stopped sipping from their Ridley cups?

"About that." Fifteen years wasn't *that* long, was it?

Jamie's gaze narrowed. "So how did you even come up with these designs if you haven't even been here in a decade and a half?"

Okay, put like that, it definitely sounded like a very long time. "Well, I don't need to be on location in order to create my designs."

Again, it was the truth. Any architect would agree, but of course Jamie had to make it sound like nothing more than an excuse.

"Because it's all the same? Just some stores to be torn down..." She waved her coffee cup at their surroundings.

He shook his head. He could see at least one shop in the far-off distance that would remain unscathed. "Not at all."

"...History to be ignored," she said sharply. Then she gave him a long, meaningful look that he felt deep in the pit of his stomach.

Were they still talking about Waterford? Because it suddenly felt like they were talking about themselves. As a couple.

Sawyer's mouth grew dry, and he was suddenly very aware of the perfect shape of her impertinent mouth. Bee-stung lips, perfectly pink, like a bow on a present, just waiting to be opened.

Then she abruptly looked away. "Beth, how long have you had your hobby warehouse?"

"Thirty-five years," Beth said.

"Thirty-five *years*," Jamie repeated, clearly for Sawyer's benefit. "People have been coming to your store for everything they need, from scrapbooking needs to their homemade Christmas decorations."

"That's right." Beth's chest puffed out a little.

Jamie was on a roll now, talking a mile a minute. There was no stopping her. Maybe he shouldn't have been so quick to provide her with complimentary caffeine. "But because of where your store is located, some people—in *Portland*—think it would make a great place for some retail, space station-like mega development, forcing you to sell your life's work. Is that right?"

Beth aimed a death glare straight at Sawyer. "It is *not*."

Even the guy Sawyer had hired to man the espresso machine was beginning to regard him with skepticism.

"No." Jamie's expression turned sweet, innocent—overly so, as if butter wouldn't melt in her mouth. "It is not."

Sawyer squirmed as all heads turned toward him. Now was the time for a rebuttal, but he couldn't seem to come up with anything that would justify putting Beth out of business or making her move to a completely new location. How was he supposed to compete with things like scrapbooking and homemade Christmas decorations? They were even more homey than cinnamon.

"It's not a space station," he finally said, a weak defense at best.

Beth and Chuck exchanged a dubious glance.

"It's not," Sawyer muttered again.

But no one seemed to be listening to him anymore.

And that's how it's done.

Jamie flashed Sawyer her sauciest grin, spun around and headed back toward her library cart. She could feel his eyes on her the entire time, but she refused to give him the satisfaction of looking back. No way. She was perfectly content to let him stew over there, neck deep in hot chocolate and lattes.

He'd really thought he could turn on the charm and convince everyone he was just a 'hometown boy' who wanted the best for Waterford? The nerve! Jamie wasn't about to let him get away with that, especially since he obviously didn't have a clue anymore about what the business district represented to the community. Free drinks couldn't replace history and tradition, any more than a dash of cinnamon could make up for fifteen years of absence. That was a lot to ask of a common household spice.

She couldn't wait to give Lucy a blow-by-blow of the conversation they'd just had. Beth and Chuck had practically been eating out of Sawyer's hand until she'd pointed out his hypocrisy. Another point scored for True Love!

But gloating was going to have to wait, because as she drew closer to the spot where Lucy was busy setting up True Love's Fire and Ice booth, she realized she wasn't the only one headed that way. As Lucy pushed the latticework backdrop into place, Rick sprinted toward her from the street corner.

"Lucy, let me help you with that." He picked up one side of the backdrop and hauled it into place.

Red and pink silk roses were tucked into the open spaces of the lattice and a swag of greenery interwoven with baby's breath and tiny pink flowers draped from one end of it to the other. Aunt Anita had helped Jamie put it together two years ago, and it still looked pristine. Lush and romantic, perfect for True Love's booth.

"Thank you." Lucy smiled up at Rick.

Jamie veered off-course and hid behind another vendor's collapsed tent so as not to interrupt what she *hoped* was the moment that Rick would finally ask Lucy out on a date. Doubtful, if past history was an indication, but a girl could dream.

"Where's Jamie?" Rick said.

"Jousting with her ex." Lucy glanced toward Sawyer's coffee cart, where a new trio of business owners had assembled around him. The man was relentless. Why couldn't he just pack his bags and move on?

Jamie's heart gave a tiny pang at the thought. Ugh, what was wrong with her?

"Sawyer has her going, huh?" Rick's mouth curved into a lopsided grin.

Lucy placed a hand on one hip. "That and trying to save the store she's loved since childhood and sunk her life's savings into."

Jamie couldn't help smiling to herself. Lucy was firmly Team Jamie, as she should be.

"There." Lucy tucked a fallen flower back in place, then turned away from the latticework to face Rick. "How do I look?"

She unbuttoned her practical trench coat to show Rick her new cashmere sweater—caramel-colored, with deep red hearts scattered all over it. Lucy had been with her when she'd bought it at a Valentine's sale at a cute boutique in the business district a few days ago.

"The only answer is: gorgeous," Rick said, as devoted as a golden retriever.

How could Lucy *not* see that he was head over heels in love with her? The mind reeled.

"Oh." Lucy's cheeks flushed pink as she

re-fastened the buttons of her coat. "Aren't you sweet?"

Jamie held her breath. It was the perfect opening for Rick to tell her how he felt. *Come on, do it.*

He cocked his head. "Why do you ask?"

Uh-oh.

"Quentin's stopping by." Lucy beamed as she unloaded a stack of books from the cart.

"Sweater Guy?" Rick said, with a heavy dose of sarcasm.

Oh, Rick. Jamie shook her head. Green-with-envy wasn't his best color.

Lucy's face fell. "It's February, Rick. People wear sweaters. *You* have sweaters."

"Yeah. But I make it look cool." He flashed her another grin, showcasing his perfect boyish dimples. Sometimes Jamie forgot Rick had been known around Waterford as a lady killer, since any time he was within a one-mile radius of Lucy, he instantly became a lovesick mess. "So, um, do you like this Quentin guy? I mean, did you have that 'wow' moment you talk about?"

Lucy blinked, visibly taken aback. Clearly there'd been no *wow.* "I don't know if I'd call it 'wow.' But he's nice...and handsome."

"Uh-huh. But no 'wow.'"

"No. I haven't had many of those." Lucy's flush was suddenly back. "Only one, actually."

This was news to Jamie. As many times as she and Lucy had discussed her dating life, she'd never mentioned having an actual, bona fide *wow* moment.

Could it have been Rick? Possibly, given the way he and Lucy were suddenly regarding one another. Something unspoken passed between them. Jamie could sense it, even from her hiding place. It felt like magic.

Lucy broke the spell first, quickly averting her gaze and busying herself with stacking and re-stacking a pile of books.

Rick cleared his throat. "What happened with that guy?"

"Nothing. Absolutely nothing happened with that guy." More stacking, more refusal to meet Rick's gaze.

He *had* to be the guy.

"You two...um...never went out?" Rick asked.

Gosh, this whole interaction was painful to watch. Jamie had to stop herself from groaning out loud.

"Nope. I thought for sure that we would, but it never happened. Maybe our timing was just off." Lucy stared down at the book in her hands. "Maybe it was all one-sided."

"So where is he now?" Rick said.

Probably standing right in front of Lucy, ask-ing obnoxious questions instead of telling her how he felt, Jamie thought.

Lucy finally met Rick's gaze again. She took a deep breath, and the magic Jamie thought she'd sensed swirling between them earlier came roaring back. It shimmered around them, as real and tangible as the brick wall currently pressed against Jamie's back.

She really needed to stop spying on people. And she would, just as soon as...

"Lucy! Hi," a voice called out, putting an abrupt halt to her train of thought. A distinctly *non*-Rick voice.

"Quentin!" Lucy waved him over to where she and Rick stood.

Oh, no.

Quentin, once again wearing a sweater, nodded at Rick. "Hi."

Rick nodded back, and just when Jamie thought the situation couldn't get any more awkward, Quentin pulled a blush-colored long-stemmed rose out from behind his back and offered it to Lucy.

"For you," he said.

Rick jammed his hands in his pockets and shifted from one foot to the other.

Lucy took the rose and held it up to her nose. Its bloom was full and vibrant, which meant it had most likely come from Anita's Flowers. "Aw, that's..." Her gaze flitted toward Rick before settling on Quentin. "Thank you."

Rick's shoulders sagged as he pointed in the direction of his bistro. "I'm gonna..."

Go make some risotto, Jamie mouthed. She would have bet money on it.

"Go make some risotto," Rick said.

Winner winner, chicken dinner.

Chapter Ten

*J*AMIE DIDN'T WANT TO INTERRUPT Lucy and Quentin, and she sure as heck didn't want to engage in another conversation with Sawyer, so she headed back toward True Love Books.

But Sawyer had other ideas, because of course he did. These days, they were never, ever on the same page. He jogged toward her from his coffee cart. She pretended not to see him, but he wasn't so easily dissuaded.

"No fair. You already know everyone in Waterford." Sawyer fell in step next to her— which was fine, once she thought about it. So long as he was walking beside her, he couldn't bribe any more business owners with his fancy beverages.

Then again, maybe he'd already blanketed the business district with hot cocoa and coffee, because as they strolled through the set-up area for the Fire and Ice Festival, a steady stream of vendors held up their Ridley cups to toast Sawyer as they grinned. Seriously? It was a wonder what kind of Ridley propaganda people would put up with in exchange for a delicious hot drink.

"Thanks, Sawyer," Sam from Kagan's Bikes said when they walked past.

"Well." The effort it took to fight back an eye roll was monumental. "It seems the 'hometown boy' is making progress."

Sawyer looked as though he were biting back a smile. "Well. You have, what? A fifteen-year head start on me."

"Six. Six years." She held up a finger, stopping him in his tracks. "I only came back to Waterford six years ago."

"Hold on." He gaped at her, mouth hanging open. It took him a beat to form words again. "You didn't come back right after college?"

She shook her head.

It seemed they'd stumbled upon yet another fact about her that he would have known if he'd kept in touch after he'd moved away. But that wasn't what people did after a break-up. Typically, they went their separate ways and never looked back.

Jamie had just never imagined that was how their story would end. It seemed unfathomable back then. Sometimes it still did...

She swallowed around the annoying lump in her throat that had yet to show any sign of going away. Was it really necessary to give Sawyer a play-by-play of everything she'd done since they'd broken up? She doubted he was actually interested.

Except the way he was looking at her made her feel like he just might be. There were questions in his warm brown eyes, questions he had no business asking. And despite everything—despite the looming town council vote, despite her very real fear that she might lose her bookstore, and despite the fact that she was so very, very angry at him—she wanted to give him the answers.

Sawyer had always been the easiest person in the world to talk to. He'd known her better than anyone, even better than Aunt Anita. And even though he'd been the quintessential popular boy and she'd just been the girl who always had her head in the clouds and her nose in a book, he'd understood her in a way that no one else ever had. Back then, or since.

But she couldn't open up to him now. If she did, she'd only end up doubly heartbroken when he left yet again—this time, after taking away the thing she loved most in the entire world.

Why, oh why, does it have to be him?

"Jamie?"

A woman's voice called her name, and for a moment, she was relieved at the interruption. Spending time alone with Sawyer wasn't a good idea, plain and simple.

But then she swiveled her head and caught sight of Mrs. Van Horn bustling toward her.

"There you are," the older woman said, glancing back and forth between Jamie and Sawyer.

"Karen." Jamie's stomach churned. "Hello."

She'd been avoiding Matt's mother for weeks because every time they saw each other, Karen tried to push Jamie into reconsidering a move to Texas. It was awkward. And now she was going to get to have that same awkward conversation *again*, but in front of Sawyer this time.

Lovely.

"I never see you anymore," Karen said, planting her hands on Jamie's shoulders and giving her a kiss on each cheek, as if they'd just bumped into each other on the streets of Paris instead of Waterford.

Jamie could feel Sawyer's amused gaze on her, and it made her face go instantly warm.

"Well, we've been busy..." she stammered.

"Being busy is the best way to get over heartbreak." Karen's expression turned mournful, as if Jamie and Matt's break-up had taken place mere days ago rather than months in the past. *Seven* months, to be exact...or had it been eight? Jamie couldn't quite remember, which was probably a sign that it hadn't been a monumental life event for her. "That's certainly been Matt's motto this past year."

Sawyer's gaze narrowed as he began eyeing the two of them with far less amusement and much more something else—something that made her heart beat hard in her chest.

The change in his expression didn't go unnoticed by Karen. She turned toward him and stuck out her hand. "I'm Karen Van Horn."

"Sawyer O'Dell." He shook her hand and smiled, but it didn't quite reach his eyes.

"Sawyer?" Karen blinked, clearly surprised—and displeased. "Jamie's ex?"

Sawyer attempted to clarify. "From a long..."

"*Long*," Jamie added.

"...time ago." He smiled.

Oh great. They were practically finishing each other's sentences now.

"I see." Karen's relief was palpable as she turned her attention back toward Jamie. "Matt talks about you all the time."

"He does?" Jamie pressed her lips together.

Why was Sawyer looking at her like that...like he *cared* if Matt thought about her all the time?

"Matt?" He arched a brow.

Karen rested a hand on her chest. "My son. Jamie and Matt dated."

Sawyer frowned. Okay, maybe he did care. Not that Jamie *cared* that he cared, because she absolutely didn't. That would be a huge mistake. People didn't go around worrying about what their sworn enemies felt toward them. It just wasn't smart.

Still, she felt the need to clarify. "A long..."

"Last year," Karen corrected.

"...time ago," Jamie finished.

Karen really needed to accept that Jamie

and Matt were over. He'd moved to Texas, and he wasn't coming back. Jamie was staying right here in Waterford, so there wasn't anything left to discuss.

Sawyer studied her through curious eyes. "A year's not *that* long ago."

Help me, she mouthed when Karen wasn't looking. If he insisted on being an observer of this uncomfortable exchange, the least he could do was make himself useful.

He took the hint, thank goodness, and made a big show of casting an apologetic glance at Karen while gesturing toward his watch. "And since we're on the subject of time, I think Jamie and I have a lunch reservation right...now."

"Yes! We do. Right now." Jamie nodded as Sawyer wrapped an arm around her and started guiding her away. As an impromptu fake lunch date, he was remarkably convincing. "It was so good to see you though. So sorry. Goodbye."

"Nice to meet you," Sawyer called with a backward wave.

And off they went with Jamie tucked beside him, close enough to see the faint scruff of a manly shadow along his jawline and to feel the warmth of his breath on her cheek when he exhaled. A rebellious little shiver worked its way up and down Jamie's spine, and she reminded herself that they'd walked this way a million times before. It was really no big deal—especially now, when they were just pretending to be together.

But her knees grew weak all the same.

Sawyer wasn't entirely sure of the plan, other than to simply get Jamie away from Matt's mother. Somehow, though, the plan seemed to involve wrapping his arm around Jamie, which had just sort of happened without him giving it any serious thought whatsoever. He'd acted purely on instinct, and once he'd done it, there was no going back.

Not that he regretted sliding his hand around her delicate waist and holding her close, because he definitely didn't. It felt good to be this close to her again. It felt *right*. He and Jamie weren't meant to be adversaries. They were meant to be something else entirely.

Something more.

Or maybe he'd simply been spending too much time thinking about the past. Waterford was like a mirror and being back had forced him to look at his life and face some uncomfortable truths. He'd missed his hometown—and that's what Waterford was, despite Jamie's mockery toward the idea of him as a "hometown boy." He'd left a piece of his heart in Waterford when he'd gone away, and he hadn't realized how much he missed it until he'd come home.

And now, walking along the banks of the duck pond in the community park behind the town square with his girl by his side, he never wanted to leave again.

She's not your girl. She hasn't been for a very long time.

He let her go, then shoved his hands in his pockets to keep himself from putting his arm around her again. Or worse, trying to hold her hand.

"So." He struggled for something to say, finally indulging his curiosity about Karen Van Horn and her son, Matt, who must be the dentist he'd heard about from Rick. "I take it she's not your biggest fan?"

Three ducks glided past them across the smooth blue surface of the lake, quacking as they went. Sawyer wished he could toss them some cracked corn or oats, like he and Jamie had done on almost every one of their lunch breaks during senior year.

"Actually, it's the opposite." Jamie let out a nervous-sounding laugh. "Yeah, if she had her way, Matt and I would be together."

Don't say it.

Do. Not. Say. It.

He cleared his throat and looked out over the water to avoid meeting her gaze. "What are the chances of that?"

Ugh, he'd said it.

"Considering he's in Texas and I'm here, I'm going to go with none." She smiled at him, then glanced over her shoulder, back toward the town square. "I think we're safe now."

Their eyes met, and they both laughed, co-conspirators in the effort to evade Matt's mother. A looseness unspooled inside Sawyer, and he felt relaxed, free. Not because they'd managed to escape, but because he and Jamie Vaughn were finally on the same side of something again.

"This reminds me of when we skipped algebra in high school," he said before he could stop himself. Thus far, she hadn't seemed too keen on trips down memory lane.

To his surprise and immense delight, she instantly lit up. "Oh! And Coach Taylor caught us."

"And you miraculously talked our way out of detention." She'd been a force to be reckoned with back then. That, at least, hadn't changed.

They passed a cluster of trees with branches hanging low, casting watercolor shadows over the lake in cool greens and blues. Sawyer's shoulder brushed against hers, and neither of them strayed farther apart.

"Well, you're not the only one who can be charming, you know." Jamie flashed him a smile that he felt clear down to his feet.

"Oh, I'm well aware of how charming you can be," he said.

So far, she'd managed to use that charm to turn what felt like the entire state of Oregon against him.

He slowed to a stop, unsure where they were

headed, both literally and metaphorically. But while they were still there, in what seemed to be a moment of truce, there was something important he needed to say. "Believe it or not, I was really happy to see you in the bookstore again, before things got so complicated."

"Complicated. That's one word for it." She nodded, still smiling, but it had gone a bit wobbly around the edges. "I was glad to see you, too."

His breath bottled up inside him for a moment. "Yeah?"

"It reminded me of how we first met."

"I don't remember you trying to bean me in the head with Jane Austen when we first met." Minor detail, but one that had almost ended with a concussion.

He laughed and she did the same.

"No, but it was in the same bookstore," she countered.

Sawyer remembered it well. "Yes, right where the romance and sci-fi/fantasy genres converge."

"Right there on the shelf—the book we were both looking for." She held out her hands as if showcasing the perfect invisible book on an invisible shelf...a shelf from another life.

"*The Princess Bride,*" they both said in unison.

"You had just arrived in Waterford," she said.

"It was my fifth town in four years." He'd always sworn that once he started making his own way in the world, he'd never move around as much as he had when he was a kid and look at his life now. *You're fixing that, though. This will be the job that changes everything.* That's why he was trying to urge the town council to vote in favor of the re-design so he could get a permanent position with Ridley and finally put down some roots. "And you were my second friend."

Jamie's face crumpled into an expression of mock despair. "Rick will always be first."

"But you'll always be prettier."

A giggle escaped her. "Don't tell him that."

"I would never. It would destroy him." He was only half joking. Rick the Romancer might have finally fallen for someone, but Sawyer had a feeling his ego was still mostly intact—and as sensitive as ever. "I've got to confess."

Jamie's face fell. She was suddenly looking at him as if he was about to make some terrible announcement, like he was planning to tear down another of her favorite buildings. Or worse, her beloved tree.

That wasn't what he had in mind at all. "I should have said something earlier, but...I'm hungry."

She laughed again, and the sound was like music to him. "Me too! I skipped breakfast."

"Lunch?" He dipped his head, searching her gaze.

They could do this, couldn't they—share a simple meal together? It didn't mean either one of them was backing down. At the end of the day, he would always be on Ridley's side and she'd remain devoted to True Love. But they could still be friends, couldn't they?

He hoped so.

Are you sure that's all you're hoping for?

Jamie bit her lip, then finally nodded. "Lunch. I know just the place."

Great! It was a date...sort of.

Wasn't it?

Chapter Eleven

*J*AMIE SHOOK HER HEAD AND snuggled her hands deep into her coat pockets as she sat across a picnic table from Sawyer at Jeff's Homemade Ice Cream. "I can't believe you're eating ice cream in this weather."

She'd brought him there for burgers, which they'd both dug into with gusto. Jeff's was famous for their cheeseburgers, and the menu hadn't changed a bit since the modest burger joint/ice cream shop opened back in the 1950s. The restaurant had a few tables inside, but she and Sawyer had *always* sat outside when they'd come back here in high school. Doing otherwise would have been out of the question—a massive breach of tradition. But with the wind blowing off of the lake and a fine silver mist clinging to the forest's tree line, she couldn't fathom eating anything frozen out there today.

Sawyer apparently had no problem with it,

as the half-empty bowl in front of him attested. He paused with his spoon halfway to his mouth, grinning like a school kid. "It's Sundae Madness! I can't believe they still have it."

She pointed back and forth between his empty burger wrapper and the huge sundae dish. "I think that was your exact order on our very first date."

"Yeah, it was," he said, scooping up another bite. So he remembered that night as well as she did. Interesting. "Oh, wow. I've missed this so much. I've been to a million other ice cream shops, but nothing compares to Jeff's."

Truer words were never spoken. "Oh, I missed it like crazy when I was in Minnesota."

"When were you in Minnesota?"

"Right after I graduated from Reed." Seeing him sitting on a park bench, holding a pink plastic spoon with Jeff's old, wooden duck-shaped sign mere feet away, was giving Jamie serious high school flashbacks. Maybe that was why the words spilled out of her easily now, just like they used to. "I did an internship at a newspaper in Minneapolis and then they made me a full-time reporter. Mostly 'human interest' stories."

"Did you like it?" he said.

"I did, yeah. I learned a lot about storytelling that way." Just not enough to finish writing a full-length book on her own...yet. "But eventually I came to realize how much I missed this place. So six years ago, when I got back, Mr. Ogilvy made me manager of the store, and then when he decided to retire, I knew I had to buy it."

"Well, that doesn't surprise me. You living outside of Oregon, however, does. I never thought you would." His frowned into the melting remains of his ice cream.

"I know. You said that when you broke up with me all those years ago." Surely he hadn't forgotten that little tidbit.

"*We* broke up with *each other*," he said, jabbing at the air with his spoon for emphasis.

She raised a dubious eyebrow. "Did we?"

"I thought we did." There wasn't an ounce of irony in his tone.

So that was the way he'd seen things all these years. He'd considered their break-up mutual, when in actuality, she'd cried herself to sleep for weeks after that devastating conversation.

Technically, he hadn't outright dumped her. He'd simply said they were too young to try and make a long-distance relationship work once he left for school. In the speech he'd given her, he'd seemed focused on all the ways it would be bad for her if they tried to stay together. He'd said that he didn't want her pining away for him back in Waterford while he was away at Columbia. He wanted her to spread her wings and do the things that made her happy.

But you *make me happy.*

It was all she'd been able to say, because it had been the truth. She'd loved Sawyer O'Dell with her whole heart. And he'd loved her too. She'd known it, but when she'd reminded him of that, all he'd told her in reply was that time was on their side—something that had meant less than nothing to her then. But looking back on it now, she remembered him saying that maybe, when the time was right, they'd find their way back to each other.

She'd been so heartbroken in the aftermath that she'd forgotten that part. That was probably a good thing. If she hadn't let go of the idea of them reuniting, she might have never moved on. But now, those words seemed fortuitous somehow.

When the time is right...

But the time wasn't right. Ridley and True Love Books aside, Sawyer was back in Waterford only temporarily—he had no intention of staying put.

"No," she replied, pulling herself out of her thoughts. *No, our breakup was absolutely not mutual...but it might have been the right decision after all.* "Look, you had a very good point. People should go out into the world. See other things. Have other experiences before they decide where they want to settle down. That's what I did, and that's how I know," she said, and she meant it. She got it now.

He put down his ice cream spoon and gave her a tender smile, visibly relieved to put this part of their past behind them.

This is nice, she thought. *See, we can be friends.*

They just couldn't be more...ever. Ridley Development wasn't the only thing standing between them. There was also the matter of simple geography.

"This is where I want to be."

Sawyer probably should have spent the day knocking on doors throughout the business district, pleading his case with the shop owners. At the very least, he should have been manning his new barista cart, chatting up the good people of Waterford when they came to set up for the festival, and reminding them that they could trust him because he was the same Sawyer O'Dell he'd been fifteen years ago. There was only one problem with that plan...

It was the truth.

He was beginning to think he might actually *be* the same Sawyer O'Dell—just as caught up in Jamie to the exclusion of everything else as he had been back then—and that wasn't part of the plan at all. This wasn't a vacation. It was a very important business trip, one that could make or break his entire future. But for some crazy reason, every time Jamie smiled at him or told him some new detail about her life or twirled a lock of her cascading hair around her fingertip the same way she used to do when lost in a book, he forgot about the re-design altogether. Back in high school, she'd been able to derail him from any action or train of thought just by looking his way. He'd assumed he'd outgrown that reaction, right along with teenage hormones. But...apparently not.

That was not good. At all.

Still, when their impromptu lunch was over and it was time for both of them to get back to work, he walked her back to True Love Books. He told himself they were both headed in the same direction anyway, so it only made sense to go with her. But the fact of the matter was that he couldn't help himself. They'd walked this path together so many times before. It just felt...*right*.

"So are you still writing?" he asked as they made their way from the shaded path of the park back through the sidewalk streets of the homey neighborhood that bordered the business district.

"Here and there." She gave a little shrug, which surprised him.

Jamie's head had always been so full of stories. It made sense that she'd bought the bookshop, but he'd also expected to discover that she'd written half a dozen books of her own by now. In her high school days, she'd filled countless notebooks with poems and short stories.

"Have you published anything?"

Jamie sighed. "Not yet."

He studied her profile as they walked past the old stone church at the corner of Main and 2nd Street. She was nibbling her bottom lip like she always did when she was unsure of herself. "Have you *tried*?"

"I haven't." She shook her head and gave him a sheepish grin.

He felt himself frown. "Why not?"

"Probably for the same reason as everybody else who writes but doesn't publish—fear of rejection." She shrugged again. "Rejection hurts."

True, but the Jamie he knew never backed down from a challenge. She certainly wasn't afraid to put her heart on the line for her bookstore.

Writing was personal, though, wasn't it? Jamie had once told him that it felt like putting her heart on paper. And if it was published, her heart would be out there for all the world to see. Maybe that was why she'd chosen journalism in college instead of pursuing her dream of writing a novel. News stories were more cut and dried, less personal. Even human-interest stories were about reporting facts instead of creating new characters and plots. Publishing a novel would have been inherently more vulnerable.

He wondered if their break-up had anything to do with her fears of rejection. He sure hoped not.

They'd already discussed their break-up, though. Oddly enough, talking to her about it at long last had felt like a closure, of sorts. He wasn't sure if he should open that door again.

Beside him, Jamie swallowed and her expression began to close like a book. In an effort to lighten the mood again, Sawyer came to a halt by a big yellow caution sign at the intersection. "Duck crossing?"

The sign had a silhouette of a mama duck and four baby ducklings, all in a row. Only in Waterford.

"Yeah. Those went in a little while ago." Jamie laughed. "Do you remember Mrs. Montenegro?"

He did indeed. She lived in a big mansion in the center of downtown Waterford and organized bird-watching walks for tourists. "The woman on Ashland Avenue."

"Exactly!" Jamie's hair whipped in the wind, and she pulled her bright pink knit scarf more tightly around her neck. "So, turns out she was buying land on the outskirts of town, just little by little, until eventually, she got the local preservation society to designate the area a bird sanctuary."

"Really?" He was interested in the duck story. But he was also thinking about how nice it would be to take Jamie's hands and warm them up with his.

"Yes. But an unforeseen result is we now have an influx of ducks." She nodded toward the duck crossing sign.

"Ducks?"

"Oh, yeah. Ducks." She spread her arms out wide. "*Hundreds* of ducks."

He laughed. It felt good to forget about Ridley for once...to just enjoy the moment with her. "And they, obviously, follow the rules of the road?"

Jamie's laughter mixed with his, and that's when he knew she wasn't thinking about the re-design anymore either. It was just the two of them. Here. Together. "Well, I don't know if they actually—"

And then, just like that, their moment ended when Chuck called out to him from across the street.

"Hey, Sawyer!" He stood in the doorway of the pizzeria and waved. "Dad wants to say hi."

Right. Because he was in Waterford to woo business owners, not his high school sweetheart.

"Um...I should..." He pointed toward the pizzeria, but his stubborn feet refused to move.

"Oh, yeah. Yeah. Go ahead." Jamie nodded, and the somewhat frozen smile on her face made him even more reluctant to abandon their walk back to True Love. But he didn't have much of a choice.

Besides, she knew the way home. She always had. Sawyer was the one who couldn't quite seem to figure that out.

He stalled for a moment longer, postponing the inevitable, until Jamie waved him on. Then he jogged across the street, where Chuck's dad was waiting for him with a welcoming smile and effusive handshake. At last, a shop owner who just might be on his side.

A wave of relief passed through Sawyer, and he told himself not to look back at Jamie lingering on the street corner. But he did it anyway, and the wistful glimmer in her true-blue eyes made his chest tighten.

Who was he kidding? She hadn't forgotten about Ridley at all. Not for a second.

The meeting at the pizzeria lasted all afternoon. It was more a reunion than an actual business discussion, but after donning an apron and proving to Chuck and his dad that he could still roll out pizza dough and toss it in the air like a pro—or at least like a reasonably competent amateur — Sawyer walked away with a promise that the pizzeria would throw their support behind the Ridley project.

Finally, a small victory. Sawyer would take them where he could get them, so when he returned to Rick's house later in the evening, he was in the mood for a little celebrating.

Perhaps not on the scale of whatever Rick had going on, though, because when Sawyer walked through the door, he found his friend sitting at the kitchen table in front of six opened bottles of wine. Jazz music drifted from the stereo speakers as Rick swirled a glass of red in his hands.

"Hey. What's all this?" Sawyer said, scanning the area for another wineglass. Nope, just the one.

Rick barely glanced up at him before picking up a pencil and jotting something down on a notepad. "I'm doing a last-minute Valentine's-themed wine tasting at the restaurant."

So. Not a party, then. But at least Rick wasn't planning on drinking all of this alone.

"What made you think of this? Oh, let me guess." Sawyer aimed finger guns at Rick. "Lucy."

"Yeah, Lucy. I saw her down at the park and we talked." Rick took a sip from his glass, and his eyes went all dopey like they always did when he talked about Lucy. "I don't know if I'm seeing what I want to see, but I feel like maybe...I mean..."

His tongue was all tied up in knots, and Sawyer knew it had nothing to do with the wine.

Still, the stammering continued. "Probably not, but..."

"*Rick.*" How many more times was he going to have to say this? "You need to tell her how you feel."

Rick took a deep breath. "Okay. So I'm going to do a wine tasting. Create a fun, friendly environment where I can tell her how I feel."

He dropped his head in his hands. Sawyer didn't believe him for a minute.

Rick looked back up. "You're going to help me out and make me look good like you did the other day?"

"You don't need me for that." Sawyer snagged a bottle of Bordeaux for himself and gave Rick a solid pat on the back.

His presence hadn't made any difference whatsoever at the cooking class. But at least he could take heart in one simple truth—he wasn't the only one whose love life was a complete and total disaster.

Chapter Twelve

THE NEXT MORNING, JAMIE TOOK advantage of a quiet hour at True Love to pop over to Anita's Flowers and get a few things off of her chest.

She'd vented to Eliot the night before, but he'd dozed off mid-rant, purring up a storm. Waking him would have just been rude, so she'd bottled everything up inside until Lucy turned up for work earlier. But every time Jamie mentioned Sawyer, Lucy's expression morphed into one of amusement, as if Jamie would be talking about Sawyer for any reason other than the proposed Ridley project. Honestly, it was like Lucy thought Jamie was spending time with him because she still had feelings for him, which was definitely *not* the case.

Then what was yesterday about, exactly?

Business.

Mostly, anyway.

Jamie paced up and down a row of potted orchids while Anita polished the deep emerald-hued leaves of a plant. She tried her best to ignore the knowing look on her aunt's face, which bore a striking resemblance to the one Lucy had worn earlier. "They were just shaking hands—just Sawyer, Chuck and Chuck's dad. Like they're old friends."

"Or former employer and employee," Anita said. *So* not helpful.

Jamie rolled her eyes. "From an eternity ago."

Seriously, what could they possibly have talked about all afternoon? According to the business district's rumor mill, Sawyer had stayed at the pizzeria for hours. Someone had even seen him *throwing pizza dough up in the air.*

What was next? Was he planning on donning a tutu and pirouetting his way over to Olga's Dance Studio?

"I remember every person I've ever employed." Anita regarded the shiny leaf in her hand and, seemingly satisfied, moved onto the next plant in the row.

"Yeah, well. You're good like that," Jamie said. Then, upon further reflection, "And so is Chuck... and Chuck's dad." That was yet another thing she loved about the business district exactly as it was.

She shook her head, as if doing so could help her focus on the real problem at hand. "It's Sawyer I'm mad at."

"Mad?" Anita abandoned her plant-polishing

efforts to turn around and aim a skeptical look in Jamie's direction.

Her face went warm.

Busted.

She wasn't necessarily angry at Sawyer. Not anymore. She felt...a lot of things, actually. Far too many to try and untangle.

"Okay, I'm frustrated. I'm not mad." She shook her head. "He is winning people over right and left. And now I think Olga's Dance Studio is going to back the proposal."

Anita's lips pursed. "Well, it's not just Sawyer's charm."

Jamie paused. That didn't sound good. "What do you mean?"

Anita held up a finger, then strode past Jamie and made her way to opposite side of the sales counter. She pulled open a drawer, retrieved a sheet of paper and slapped it on the countertop.

Oh, no. Not another one.

"Is that...?" A flier. This was one white instead of blue, but it had Ridley's logo in the upper left-hand corner. Jamie recognized it from the paper cups at Sawyer's coffee and hot chocolate stand.

Anita nodded. "Mm-hmm. Twenty percent increase from their last offer."

Jamie's head spun as she scanned the words on the page. It was official—Ridley had upped its buyout offer by twenty percent.

This changed everything. The initial offer had already been generous enough that most of the business owners Jamie spoke with had been at least tempted to accept the deal, and now Ridley had gone and sweetened the pot.

She felt like she might be sick.

"I'm not going to accept it." Anita held up her hands.

Jamie shook her head. The effort it took to keep her chin from quivering was monumental, but she couldn't ask her aunt to turn down such a large sum of money. She just couldn't. "Aunt Anita."

"No. This is my home, and this store is still my joy. Besides, I'm too young to retire just yet." She reached out to give Jamie's hand a reassuring pat.

As relieved as Jamie was to hear that her aunt still didn't want to accept Ridley's offer, she still felt sick to her stomach. "Yeah, but if you got that, it means the others did too."

Anita nodded.

Their troubles had just gotten exponentially worse. Jamie let her head fall backward and she groaned. "Ugh."

There was one thing to do—go straight to the other business owners and try her best to persuade them to reject the deal. Wasn't that what Sawyer was doing—but from the other side?

Two could play at that game. She might not know how to toss a pizza in the air, but her passion for the business district was unparalleled.

Maybe everyone just needed to be reminded why the neighborhood needed to be saved.

She could do definitely do that. Actually, she *had* to, because the only way they were going to be able to convince the town council to vote against the re-design was by standing together as a united front.

She darted back to True Love Books, fired up the espresso machine and then left again, holding as many Valentine's-flavored lattes she could carry. Sawyer wasn't the only one who had access to caffeine. Jamie's lattes had plenty of it, and *hers* came with a dash of raspberry creme.

Sure enough, she managed to lure a few folks out of their shops for a spontaneous business meeting by one of the charming little benches that lined the streets of the district—benches slated to be demolished under Sawyer's minimalist, IKEA-like plans.

Aunt Anita sat down on the bench, while Olga, Beth and Chuck stood sipping their coffees. Jamie took a deep breath, ready to plead her case, but Olga cut her off.

Not the greatest of starts.

"It's a good offer, Jamie." Olga pulled her copy of the flier from the pocket of the camel coat she wore over her pink tights and ballet clothes.

Beth nodded. "I could pay off my second mortgage."

"And aren't we just delaying the inevitable?" Chuck asked.

Getting him to join their conversation at all had been a major victory. He'd only agreed to show up after Jamie offered to try her hand at pizza-tossing. Desperation at its finest.

"No. No, the vote on the fourteenth is to see if the council recommends going forward with the project. We stop it there, and it's done." They could nip this entire thing in the bud with one simple meeting. It was really the only way to get rid of Ridley. And Sawyer, obviously, but she couldn't think about that now. It was too confusing. "We all stick together and we say 'no,' we actually can sway the council's vote."

"I know Councilwoman Baker is in favor of it going forward," Chuck said, as if the matter was already decided. "And her husband owns Golf Mart over on Third Street. Now that's a big chunk of land."

Not ideal, but they still couldn't just roll over and let Ridley win.

"All of us together is even more land, more property, more voices," Jamie said, hating the note of desperation in her voice, but she couldn't seem to keep it at bay. "How many of you all remember what happened at Tanner Falls?"

A collective groan went up from everyone assembled. Jamie had managed to home in on a sore point. "How many of those store owners didn't even have a place to go back to? Or a place they could even recognize?"

The area had been completely demolished.

Shops that sold antiques that had been in place for over a hundred years were gone, replaced with a tech store and hipster hangouts that sold moustache wax, acai bowls and hemp-infused dog treats. Not that Jamie had anything against hipsters. Hipsters were lovely. Hipsters got excited about things like manual typewriters and crocheting and avocado toast, all things Jamie adored as well. It just wasn't the same, having everything trendy and soulless, aimed at a generic "type," in a town where the shops used to be charming and full of unique character. What's worse, when the new development took over, the original shop owners who'd been in business in Tanner Falls for years had no place else to go. They'd been forced to either retire or move to an entirely new city.

No one wanted that to happen in the town they loved so much.

"We all want what's best for Waterford. We understand the importance of bringing in new people to our district. It's why we started the Fire and Ice Festival," she said. They couldn't give up. The festival was just days away, and it seemed to draw more and more people to the area every year.

If the festival didn't do the trick and put a stop to the redevelopment talks, perhaps the best way to persuade the others to take a stand against Ridley was to remind them how much their businesses meant to them.

"Look, you all know how much I loved my

bookstore, even before it was mine." She pressed her hands to her heart. True Love Books was a part of her. Without it, she'd be lost, and she knew she couldn't be the only one who felt that way about his or her business. "But I believe all of you love your stores just as much."

A hush fell over their little group, until Olga reached out to squeeze Jamie's hand. "I've been in the same dance studio for over twenty years. I don't know where I'd be without it."

"Right. And if we are all one voice at that council vote, maybe you won't have to, Olga," Jamie said.

Hope fluttered inside her. Maybe, just maybe, her words were starting to sink in. She searched the faces of her friends surrounding her, and there was a newfound spark of determination in just about everyone's expression.

With one exception. "What's on your mind, Chuck?"

He looked far too sheepish all of a sudden and couldn't seem to bring himself to meet her gaze.

Please, please, please don't let that mean what I think it means.

Chuck took a deep, pained breath and finally looked her in the eye. "Well..."

The morning after his lunch date with Jamie and the meeting at the pizzeria, Sawyer was back in the business district, ready to continue his campaign to win hearts and change minds. Now that he had at least one business owner on his side, he hoped others would follow.

The council members would be the ones casting the actual votes, but the thought of the town council going forward with the project against opposition from the shop keepers made his stomach churn. He knew he shouldn't feel that way—not when he firmly believed that the plan was the best thing for Waterford. If the re-design didn't go through, the business district's slow decline would continue and all the shops would close, one by one, until there was nothing left. He'd seen this kind of thing happen over and over again. Revitalizing areas like Waterford was part of his job, and he was quite good at it. The project should be a home run for everyone. The shop owners would get a generous buyout, the town would get a bustling business district again, and he'd get just the kind of job he'd been hoping for.

And yet, he couldn't find a way to feel totally comfortable with the situation. Maybe because the line between personal and business was becoming blurrier by the second. He cared about this town in a way that he'd never cared about another project before—and he cared about the people involved...maybe more than he should.

Yesterday had been a good day, though. A very good day. Chuck and his dad had seen the light, which meant things were finally looking up and there was a chance he could get his job done without breaking any hearts.

Other than the most important one of all.

An ache settled in the back of his throat every time he thought about Jamie. He told himself she could rebuild. She could reopen True Love Books in one of the retail spaces of the multi-use complex he'd planned. Or if she truly couldn't stand his design—and part of him winced at that thought—she could find a new location. But he'd been in town for days already and she was more resolute than ever. She'd never give up her original bookshop without a fight.

Sawyer stopped in front of Waterford's old theatre building to admire its architecture—its stone facade and rough-hewn arched doorway. He'd always been passionate about the details that made up a building. He loved the way that simple things like brick and mortar came together to form something bigger and grander than the sum of its parts. The pieces of Waterford came together in a way that he'd always found beautiful and special. But that didn't mean change was necessarily bad. He just needed to keep reminding himself that what he was doing was a good thing. The *right* thing.

Whether Jamie agreed with him or not.

He resumed walking, picking up his pace, but his cell phone rang before he reached the next street corner. He dug around in the pocket of his peacoat for it and, for a split second, fantasized that maybe the call would be from her.

It wasn't, of course.

Dana's name lit up the screen instead, and when he answered the call, she launched into a discussion without bothering to say hello. "Chuck Blevins from the pizza place sent in his agreement this morning."

She must have been calling him during a mid-morning Starbucks run, because Sawyer could hear the hum of Portland's city streets in the background—cars slicing through the rain, honking horns, jackhammers. All things notably absent where he stood right now. "That's good news."

"He liked the idea of one of his dad's old employees being in charge of the redesign," she said. Then she added a rare, "Good job."

He should have been thrilled. The contract made things official—Chuck and his dad were on board, which meant Sawyer was one step closer to the permanent job he desperately wanted at Ridley. But as he stood talking to Dana, his gaze drifted across the street where he noticed Jamie and Anita talking to a small group of other business owners. They all had paper cups in their hands—non-Ridley cups, he noted—but judging from their glum expressions, it wasn't merely a casual coffee date.

"How's it going with the bookstore?" Dana said.

He gave a start. He'd forgotten he was in the middle of a call. "Jamie and I are talking."

It was the truth, technically. Plus, he really wanted to try and keep Jamie out of Dana's crosshairs.

But of course, she pressed for specifics. "About her supporting the project?"

Across the street, Jamie and her group disbanded. Chuck Blevins was the first to leave, walking in the direction of the pizzeria with his head bowed and shoulders hunched. The others followed suit, Olga and Beth going their separate ways while Jamie and Anita walked together, arm in arm.

"It's a work in progress," he muttered under his breath.

Dana's tone took on a distinct note of displeasure. "As long as there *is* progress before the council vote. There's a reason Ridley chose you for this."

He was well aware of the reason. He was also aware that Jamie and Anita both looked visibly shaken, and he was pretty sure that his very presence in Waterford as a Ridley representative was the root cause of their distress. His pizzeria conquest suddenly didn't feel much like a victory anymore.

He swallowed hard. "I remember."

The rest of the day passed in a blur for Jamie as she went through the motions of smiling at customers, helping them choose books, and keeping up her usual level of animated chatter.

True Love Books had always been Jamie's happy place. She loved her customers...but today she just wasn't feeling it. All she could think about was her conversation with Anita, Olga, Beth and Chuck earlier, and the horrible sense of dread that had settled in the pit of her stomach since she'd learned Chuck had signed the paperwork to sell his property to Ridley.

She couldn't believe he'd caved. Now all the other businesses in the district would probably fall like dominoes until she'd eventually be forced to close her doors. The worst-case scenario suddenly seemed like a very real possibility.

At the end of the day, she locked the doors, slipped into her red swing coat and placed Eliot's cat carrier on the counter, dreaming of a bubble bath and a rom-com movie. Anything to get her mind off of the proposed Ridley project.

And Sawyer O'Dell. Because, really. Weren't the two just about synonymous at this point?

"Eliot?" She leaned over the counter but couldn't spot her kitty anywhere until he popped up onto the countertop, seemingly from out of nowhere.

Meow.

She scratched behind his ears and he purred, long and loud.

"Aw, good boy." Jamie held him up so that the

two of them were eye to eye. "Okay, Eliot. What'll we do if we can't save this place, huh?"

Eliot blinked his glittering cat eyes, taking it all in. Jamie couldn't imagine what he would do all day if he couldn't come to True Love. He was much too social to be stuck at home all day. If the store closed, numerous people, plus the world's sweetest cat, would suffer. Not just Jamie.

But she couldn't think about that right now. She'd been thinking of little else all day, to no avail. Right then, she just needed a break from it all.

"There you go, bud." She tucked Eliot inside his carrier and zipped it up tight, for once anxious to get home and try to forget about True Love for a while.

But as she reached for her keys in the flow-ered china dish by the register, her gaze snagged on The Story of Us box. She'd tucked it by the register so she could read the rest of Mary and Harris's letters, but she hadn't found the time. Maybe a little non-fiction romance reading was just what she needed tonight.

She slid the box toward her and flipped it open. Just one letter, then she and Eliot would go home for some serious couch time.

Darling Mary. Words alone cannot express how grateful I am that you did not listen when I told you not to write. Each story you relay to me of the people

*back in Waterford reminds me anew what
it is I'm fighting for—it is love.*

How could she stop there? Impossible...

An hour later, post-bubble bath and tucked
under her favorite flannel blanket in her pink
heart–patterned pajamas, she opened the next.
And then the next.

Each one was a love letter, not only between
two people who'd fallen for each other, heart and
soul, but also to the people of Waterford...to the
town itself.

> *Though we have been apart for what
> feels like ages, my love for you remains
> ever steadfast, ever true. Please keep
> the stories coming, my dear. Your words
> inspire me and bring me hope.*
>
> *Love,*
>
> *Harris*

Once Jamie had read them all, she started
over again from the beginning. She wished the
town council could see all of these heartfelt
words. She wished *everyone* in Waterford could.
Maybe then they wouldn't be so quick to erase
over a hundred years of the community's history.

Wait.

She sat up straight, heart pounding with
adrenaline. A sleepy Eliot peeked at her through
heavy eyelids.

There *was* a way for everyone to see these

letters, and Jamie knew precisely how to make it happen. She searched for her cell phone among the folds of her blanket until she found it, then fired off a text to Lucy.

Meet me at the bookstore early. I have an idea.

Chapter Thirteen

A GOOD NIGHT'S SLEEP AND ABOUT a thousand photocopies later, Jamie felt completely reinvigorated and ready to fight for True Love.

After giving Lucy a rundown of the letters, they'd zipped over to the mail center down the street to make copies of the two most sentimental missives between Mary and Harris and purchase stacks of pink and gray envelopes. Then they came back to the store and formed a two-person assembly line to get the copies folded and inserted into the envelopes. Copies of Mary's letter went into the pink envelopes while Harrison's went into the gray ones.

"So, we're going to keep half the copies of these letters here and take the other half to the Fire and Ice Festival," Jamie said, reaching for the embossing stamp and sealing wax they were using to give the letters the perfect vintage touch.

"Bring people from there to here." Lucy grinned.

Jamie nodded. "And here to there."

"So they can read what happens next." Lucy finished stuffing her stack of envelopes and reached for more.

The Fire and Ice Festival was the perfect opportunity to showcase the letters. The festival brought more people to the area than any other Waterford event, plus the timing was perfect because the town council vote on the Ridley design was scheduled for February fourteenth. Since the festival took place right before Valentine's Day, Mary and Harrison's letters would have maximum impact.

Jamie got chills just thinking about it. Mary and Harrison had been the original owners of the bookshop, and now they just might be the ones who ended up saving True Love. She couldn't imagine a better happily-ever-after ending.

Joy welled up in her heart. They could do this—they could save the business district. "Exactly. Yeah, I want these letters to inspire people and help them reconnect with the town's history. Maybe then they'll be less eager to tear it down."

Her hands stilled as another idea hit her, and the envelope she was holding fluttered to the floor.

Lucy cocked her head. "What are you thinking?"

"I'm thinking..." She was thinking a lot of

things. Since the Ridley people and their blue flier rolled into town, her mind had been spinning so fast, she could barely keep up. But right this second, she was thinking that maybe the residents of Waterford and the town council weren't the only ones who needed to reconnect with the town's history. There was someone else who needed to embrace the city's roots, to rediscover everything that made Waterford so special.

And what better way to do it than a trip down memory lane? Not just a figurative one, but an actual tour through the cobblestone streets and old brick buildings that told Waterford's story. And *their* story.

She bit her lip and cast a pleading glance at Lucy. "Can you watch the store a while?"

She hated to ask. They had so much on their plate already, but as usual, Lucy was more than ready to step up to the plate.

"Yeah." She shrugged as if it were no big deal.

But it was. Lucy's friendship was precious, and Jamie didn't even want to think about what it might be like to not see her every day at True Love.

Of course, if her plan worked out the way she intended, she wouldn't have to give that up. She gave Lucy a quick hug, grabbed her coat and darted for the door. "Thank you."

The Oregon air smelled like pine and felt cool on her face as she made her way down the sidewalk, dialing Sawyer's number as she went. She tried not to think about the fact that she'd some-how managed to memorize his cell number since he'd been back in town or that she'd had to stop herself from dialing it a few times.

Waterford felt different, now that Sawyer was back. Jamie woke up every morning feeling alive in a way she hadn't in a very long time, the day stretching before her like an enchanted, shim-mering world of possibility. She knew it didn't make sense. The future—specifically, *her* future and the future of True Love—was anything but certain right now. Waking up feeling like an anvil had been placed dead in the center of her chest would have made more sense.

But she couldn't quite help it. Truthfully, she'd enjoyed every moment she'd spent with Sawyer in the past few days, even the moments they'd spent arguing. It boggled the mind.

She refused to let that enjoyment distract from her mission, though. She and Sawyer were *not* Mary and Harrison. The most important thing was saving True Love—way more important than any doomed attempt at a relationship with Saw-yer. She could tell that Sawyer was beginning to reconnect with Waterford, though. She'd even been fool enough to believe that his recent pizza-tossing episode had been a simple sentimental exercise instead of a way to persuade Chuck and his dad to succumb to the dark side.

Still, he seemed more and more at home there every day. If she could just get him to see that

Waterford was truly worth saving just as it was, she knew he'd come around. She wasn't sure when exactly it had happened—probably some-time around the moment she'd witnessed him feasting on Sundae Madness at Jeff's—but she'd come to the conclusion that deep down, he was still the same Sawyer O'Dell she'd fallen in love with. He just didn't know it.

All Jamie needed to do was remind him...

Without accidentally falling in love with him all over again in the process.

No problem at all.

She'd have to be the biggest fool in the world to make that mistake.

Sawyer didn't have a clue why Jamie wanted him to drop everything he was doing and meet her at town hall, but he was ninety-nine percent certain it didn't have anything to do with signing the Rid-ley offer.

Make that one hundred percent. He knew Ja-mie well enough to know that she'd never, ever turn her back on True Love. Still, he did indeed drop everything he was doing the minute she called. Dana had made it expressly clear that he was supposed to keep the lines of communica-tion with Jamie open. He didn't have much of a choice.

Keep telling yourself that, he thought as he jammed his hands in the pockets of his puffer vest and crisscrossed the quaint maze of blocks in the business district, making his way toward Jamie. He wasn't Ridley's lackey. He wasn't even an employee yet, so he definitely had a choice in the matter. Like so many times before, he simply chose Jamie.

He was beginning to suspect that he always would.

Dial it down, Romeo. She didn't ask you to run off into the sunset with her. This probably isn't even a date.

The realization was surprisingly disappointing. Still, his breath hitched when he spotted her standing in the street with her face tipped upward, blond waves tumbling down her back as she gazed at the old church's spire. The reverence in her eyes made his heart hurt. And he was suddenly very glad his hands were safely buried in his pockets to prevent him from acting on the crazy impulse he had to bury his hands in her hair and kiss her right there in the middle of the street.

He slowed to a stop a few feet away, content to just watch her for a brief, unguarded moment—a sacred sliver of time in which neither of them was hiding behind an agenda. It was as excruciating as it was precious, mainly because he didn't want it to end.

Then she turned and smiled at him—the most

open, easy smile she'd bestowed him since he'd stepped back into her life. For a split second, he was seventeen again.

"Thanks for meeting me." She squared her shoulders, preparing for battle, and the moment vanished as quickly as it had appeared.

He nodded, not quite trusting himself to speak when there was suddenly an aching hole in the place where his heart used to be.

"This used to be your favorite building in Waterford." Her gaze flitted back to the town hall's sturdy brick and aged yellow clapboard. "You drew it all the time."

He stepped closer until they were shoulder-to-shoulder, both gazing in the same direction for once. "I did it in watercolors, too. It always reminded me of someplace grand."

"Well, it originally was a church," she said in her best tour guide voice. "And now it has been repurposed to be a town hall and a theatre."

Sawyer was beginning to get an idea what her surprise invitation had really been about.

She tilted her head and studied him in a way that made his pulse kick up a notch. "You know, you say you're a 'hometown boy,' but did you actually miss your hometown while you were away?"

"Honestly?" He didn't realize how ashamed he was of the truth until he had to say it out loud. "I've been too busy with work or looking for the next project to do much of anything else."

Jamie didn't judge him, though. That had never been her style. Instead, she twirled in a quick little spin on her toes and waved at him to follow her. "Then let me remind you of what you left behind."

Okay, then.

Sawyer jogged to catch up with her, and what followed could only be described as a determined effort on Jamie's part to reacquaint him with every square inch of Waterford, with no stone left unturned.

They started at the duck pond, where a pair of cruiser bicycles were waiting for them. One of them belonged to Jamie and the other looked suspiciously like one Sawyer had seen recently in Rick's garage. Sawyer couldn't remember the last time he'd ridden a bike that hadn't been bolted to the floor of a gym. He climbed aboard and pedaled after Jamie, appreciating the difference within seconds. The wind rippled through his hair, numbing his face as they made a wide loop around the water, weaving in and around oak trees, branches tipped green with the promise of new spring growth.

They zipped past couples walking hand-in-hand and parents with small children whose fingertips were nestled in homemade knitted mittens—the kind Sawyer's grandmother had made for him when he was a boy. The old lampposts lining the path had been painted bright cherry-red since he'd moved away, and new park benches perched at the water's edge. Ducks lingered nearby, waiting for someone to take a seat and toss them some cracked corn.

From the duck pond, they made their way to the park, traveling down the bike lane that hugged Main Street. Jamie's hair streamed behind her in lustrous gold ribbon as she led the way.

They parked their bikes beneath the shade of a willow tree swaying in the gentle Pacific breeze, and Jamie surprised him with a picnic lunch hidden in the wicker basket hanging from her bike's handlebars. He could tell at first glance that Rick had nothing to do with the meal. Instead of gourmet fare, they dined on PB&J, apples and kettle chips, which had been the exact lunch Jamie always brought to school in a brown paper sack. It was the best meal he'd tasted in years, even though swallowing proved difficult with such an aching longing in his throat.

Next up was a walk through the tea garden on the banks of the old waterlily pond, as breathlessly beautiful as a Monet painting. Huge orange and white koi fish splashed at their feet, and the water seemed to dance with silvery light. A tour of Waterford wouldn't have been complete without a stop at True Love, though, which Jamie saved for the grand finale.

The shop had long closed by the time they arrived, but the courtyard was lit with the welcoming glow of hundreds of twinkling fairy lights.

Jamie wound her hair into a slouchy cashmere beanie and grinned at him as she took a seat at the café table closest to the fountain, where flowers floated in the water, swirling with pink and red petals.

Sawyer sat down opposite her and tried to remind himself that they weren't on a date. She'd been perfectly honest about her intentions, and they were in no way romantic. She was on a mission to remind him what he'd left behind when he'd moved away from Waterford.

Mission accomplished.

A keen sense of loss burrowed deep in his gut—an open wound that somehow felt as fresh as if he'd packed up and walked away yesterday instead of fifteen years ago. He'd missed this place more than he'd realized, but it was more than that. He'd missed *her*.

He still missed Jamie.

He wouldn't have thought it possible to miss someone who was right there, close enough to touch, but it was. He missed the warmth of the small of her back against his palm. He missed the smell of her hair, cool and lush, like frosted rose petals. He missed kissing her...of course he did.

But most of all, he missed knowing she was his. She wasn't anymore, and it was all his fault. He couldn't blame Eric the councilman for his interest in her, nor could he blame Matt the dentist. He couldn't even blame the past, because the real barrier standing between them didn't have anything to do with choices they'd made yesterday. The biggest problem was firmly rooted in the here and now.

He balled his hands into fists under the table and tried not to imagine them tearing down her bookstore, brick by beloved brick. He was so caught in that image that it startled him when Jamie slid something toward him. It was the box—the one from the newspaper article with *The Story of Us* printed across the front, like the title of a book. Jamie glanced down at it, so he opened the lid and found a bundle of old letters inside.

Sawyer read them, one by one, in the soft light of the courtyard. At first, he kept glancing up at Jamie, because it felt strange reading such private correspondence between two people who were clearly very deeply in love while she watched. There were more than a few parallels between Mary and Harrison and himself and Jamie. Surely she'd noticed.

But the more he read, the more lost he became in their story. And it wasn't until he reached the end and their fate became clear that he was able to breathe again.

At last, he looked back up.

Jamie took a deep breath and motioned toward the fragile paper in his hand. "They wrote to each other throughout his time away in the war. And then when he got back, they started True Love books. Her father originally owned this building, but Harris loved books so much he got the entire property and the rest is…"

Her voice drifted off, and Sawyer finished for her. "History."

Jamie nodded. "Mm-hmm."

He glanced around, and even though he'd known True Love for as long as he'd known Jamie, it felt like he was seeing it—*really* seeing it—for the very first time. "This is just such a special place. The store, the courtyard, the tree…"

It towered above them, its branches shimmering in the moonlight.

"I've always thought so. And then to find these Valentines from old customers—I mean, people who went out, picked out a card and wrote in their appreciation for True Love Books." She sighed. "It just makes it that much more special."

Their gazes locked, and a deep calm came over him. For the first time since he'd come home, it finally felt like they were seeing eye to eye. Maybe…just maybe…

Sawyer's pulse thundered in his ears. Was it crazy that he was thinking about kissing her again? Probably. Yet even though he knew it was a terrible idea, he couldn't help but wonder if she was thinking about it too. Yes. Yes, she was. He would have bet his life on it. Her cheeks flushed pink, and then her lips parted, and all of Sawyer's breath stalled in his lungs.

Then Jamie's cell phone vibrated its way across the table, severing the invisible, delicate thread that had somehow connected them to-gether again.

She flipped the phone over to glance at the screen, and Matt's name flashed on the display.

"You can take that if you want. I can..." Saw-yer held up a hand, surrendering before he'd even begun to fight for her. He had no right. Not when he was actively involved in the destruction of everything she held near and dear.

"Um, no." She flipped the phone back over. "No."

Sawyer studied her, but he couldn't get a read on her expression. She'd closed up again, just like one of the books she loved so much.

"Were you ever tempted?" He nodded toward her phone as it stopped vibrating. "To go to Texas with Matt, start over someplace new?"

"A little," she said, and her smile turned bit-tersweet. "But I couldn't tell if it was because of how I felt for him or if I was just..."

"Lonely?" Sawyer guessed. He knew the feel-ing well.

"Reliving not going to Columbia with you way back when," she corrected.

Sawyer sat back in his chair, genuinely sur-prised. He'd never realized that had been an op-tion. "Do you wish you had?"

She arched a brow. "Do you wish you'd stayed?"

Right this second? *Yes.* He bit down hard on his tongue to keep himself from saying it.

"Don't answer that." Jamie shook her head. "Really?"

This conversation had begun to feel like the heart-to-heart they should have had fifteen years ago. Maybe it was time to be fully honest with each other and put all their cards on the table.

"I mean, you didn't stay and I didn't go, and because of those decisions, we are who we are today," she said, and in way, it was the most honest truth of all.

But it did nothing to relieve the empty feeling in the pit of Sawyer's stomach. If anything, he felt worse, because he'd just experienced his best day in recent memory, and throughout it all, Jamie's words from the beginning of the tour had been swirling in his mind.

Let me remind you of what you left behind.

He gave her his most tender smile. "Well, for what it's worth, I think you turned out pretty well."

"Yeah?" She brightened, lightening the mood. "Jury's still out on you." Then she pulled a face and winked, so he'd know she was only kidding.

But in the end, Sawyer wasn't so sure.

Chapter Fourteen

SAWYER SPENT THE FOLLOWING DAY manning his caffeine cart and chatting up local shop owners. With the Fire and Ice Festival just days away, business was brisk. The booths at the town square were really taking shape, and Sawyer's street corner was right in the center of things. In between handing out flavored lattes and hot chocolate, he helped unload boxes from nearby trucks and nailed signage in place. The hum of activity kept him busy enough to keep his thoughts from straying to Jamie Vaughn.

Mostly.

He kept sneaking glances in the direction of True Love Books, but never caught sight of her. He told himself it was just as well. They both had work to do, and since a large portion of that work involved systematically trying to undermine one another, common sense told him that they shouldn't be spending any more time together. As lovely as yesterday had been, it hadn't changed anything. Jamie was still planning on doing everything in her power to save True Love and keep the Waterford Business District exactly as it was, and Sawyer was still trying to persuade the shop keepers and the town council to approve Ridley's re-design.

Still, every time he caught a glimpse of blond hair or polka dots out of the corner of his eye, he whipped his head around. They were never her, though. They were just Jamie-esque mirages— products of his own wishful thinking.

He really needed to get a handle on himself. Ridley was his client. With any luck, he'd have a permanent job there once the Waterford project was officially approved. Jamie had managed to convince him that True Love Books was more special than he'd realized, but he couldn't do anything about saving it. His hands were tied.

So really, from now on, they'd be better off avoiding each other. Spending time together would only lead to trouble. At least that's what he told himself until later that evening when the time for Rick's wine tasting rolled around.

He'd only been joking when he'd told Rick he wasn't going. Of course Sawyer would be there to try and help his friend out with Lucy. Rick most definitely needed it, so Sawyer was one of the very first guests to arrive.

Rick had set aside about half of the restaurant for the wine event. Cheese platters and fresh flowers covered just about every surface, and red and white cellophane bags of hand-crafted chocolates were waiting by the exit as parting gifts. Decked out in a new suit instead of his chef's whites, Rick busied himself lining up an extensive offering of wines—from crisp, cold whites to fragrant, full-bodied reds and everything between.

Sawyer watched him and tried his best not to sigh. The poor guy. If Rick would just put half as much effort into actually expressing his feelings to Lucy as he did in trying to manufacture the perfect environment in which to woo her, they'd probably be engaged by now.

At least she'd shown up. That was something. Glass in hand, Lucy perused the wine selection while Sawyer peered past her, hoping she'd come with Jamie. Those two were thick as thieves. But alas, Lucy had arrived all on her own. Good news for Rick, obviously.

Not so much for Sawyer.

You're trying to avoid Jamie from now on. Remember?

He was. Definitely.

But then he caught another flash of golden hair in his periphery, and this time it was no mirage. It was Jamie—walking into the room wearing soft pink silk and looking more beautiful than Sawyer had ever seen her.

He forgot instantly about all the ridiculous promises he'd made to himself about keeping his distance from her. He couldn't do any such thing. Nor did he want to.

Their eyes met, and Sawyer was vaguely aware of Anita's presence alongside Jamie, watching the way they stared at one another with keen interest. Jamie's lips curved into a shy smile, and it was then that Sawyer realized he hadn't been imagining things last night. Something had changed between them in the glittering courtyard. Something *real*. He wasn't sure what it might mean for the future or for their respective careers, but for once, he didn't care about that.

Ridley could wait.

He waved at Jamie, and she waved back. Then a hand landed firmly on Sawyer's shoulder—Rick's hand—and Sawyer had no choice but to switch into wingman mode.

"Oh, yeah." He turned to face Rick. "Now's your shot."

Rick paled a little, so Sawyer aimed finger guns at him in a dorky attempt to help him relax. "Be cool."

Rick rolled his eyes. "Yeah."

Sawyer patted him on the back and gave him a small shove in Lucy's direction. While Rick slowly made his way toward her, Sawyer snuck a glance at Jamie. Anita poured her a glass of red. She accepted it, then returned Sawyer's look. Once he had her attention, he nodded subtly toward Rick and Lucy. Since Jamie was such a fan of true love, he figured she'd want to witness the moment when Rick finally told Lucy how he felt.

Jamie turned her gaze toward them, eyes wide.

"Hey, Luce," Rick said.

Lucy smiled. "Hi."

Sawyer nodded to himself. So far, so good.

"You said you liked that Chardonnay last time you were here." Rick gestured toward the bottle in Lucy's hand. "Unoaked."

Lucy tipped her head to the side. "You remembered?"

Sawyer and Jamie shared a small smile from across the room.

"I remember all sorts of things." Rick flashed Lucy one of his Rick the Romancer grins. "Like the first time that we met—August ninth, two years ago. You'd only been in town for a week and you walked in here wearing a purple paisley shirt and ordered a salmon miso. With unoaked Chardonnay."

"And I remember you were hilarious." Lucy did a little hair flip, which Sawyer saw as a definite sign of progress. But then she deadpanned, "And dating Megan the Model."

Ouch.

Rick waved a dismissive hand. "We broke up."

"Ten months later." Lucy took a smooth, unoaky sip from her glass.

Sawyer decided right then and there that he liked Lucy. A lot. Rick needed someone who would challenge him instead of the type who fawned all over him. They'd be great together. The only problem was that Rick had never had to actually work for a woman's affections before. He needed more than a wingman—he needed a coach.

He cast a pleading look toward Sawyer.

Don't give up now. Did Sawyer need to give Rick a literal playbook? If Lucy had taken note of the timing surrounding his break-up, surely that meant she was interested in him. Sawyer shot him an urgent get-back-in-the-game look.

Rick took a deep breath and turned back toward Lucy, just in time to see Sweater Guy running toward them.

Sawyer groaned inwardly. Seriously? *Now?*

"Sorry, sorry! Consults ran late." Quentin kissed Lucy on both of her cheeks, European style. Sawyer would definitely be hearing about that later. "Hey, Rick."

Rick sighed and gestured vaguely toward the kitchen. "Um, I gotta go."

Lucy arched a brow. "Make some risotto?"

Sawyer almost choked on his Bordeaux.

Rick gritted his teeth. "Pour some wine."

Then he retreated back toward Sawyer's table while Lucy poured Quentin—who was indeed dressed in another sweater—a glass of the aforementioned unoaked Chardonnay. Oh, the irony.

"Maybe you shouldn't arrange any more Valentine's gatherings," Sawyer muttered once Rick reached his side.

"No. Not at all," Rick said tersely, then he smoothed down his tie and stalked toward a table in the corner where Lucy and Quentin were settling in. Rick helped them get seated but stole the romantic flower arrangement right off the center of their table as he left.

Another Valentine's Day event, another disaster. It was becoming a thing.

Sawyer shoved his hands in his pockets and leaned against the bar while trying to get a read on the Lucy/Quentin situation. Was she really into him? Did she want to someday be Mrs. Sweater Guy?

Sawyer couldn't see it. He was contemplating what Rick's next move should be when Jamie slid in next to him. The little furrow in her forehead told him she was thinking about the very same thing.

"What if we sent Lucy a Valentine from Rick? Telling her how he feels?" he murmured, still focusing on the distinct lack of chemistry going on at the Sweater table.

Jamie gasped. "Invade his privacy?"

She had a point. This was real life, not a romcom. "Fine, fine, fine. No scheming. We'll just let him continue to pine for her while gently encouraging him to reveal his feelings."

Because that was going so well.

Jamie shrugged, but looked about as convinced as Sawyer felt. "Well, it's the mature course of action."

They both laughed at the absurdity of the situation, and then Jamie pulled a pink cashmere scarf from her pocket and wound it around her neck. Sawyer had been so caught up in the Rick drama that he hadn't noticed she'd slipped into a wraparound coat—winter white, like the lacy trim on a Valentine.

He felt himself frown. "Heading home?"

"The Fire and Ice Festival starts tomorrow so this hometown girl's gotta get ready." She winked at him.

"So does this hometown boy." It was true. Mostly. "Mind a little company on the walk?"

"Not at all," she said, as if the past fifteen years had never happened and it was perfectly normal for Sawyer to walk her home.

He placed his hand on the small of her back and escorted her to the door. Outside, the air swirled with gentle raindrops, and the wet pavement shimmered like a watercolor painting. It felt like they were stepping into a misty memory, a dream. And when Jamie pulled an umbrella from her bag, Sawyer opened it for her and they huddled beneath it together, a shelter from the storm.

If she was willing to pretend, then so was he.

Jamie's plan to remind Sawyer of everything he liked best about Waterford without accidentally falling for him wasn't going quite as well as she'd planned.

Especially the second part.

She'd tucked herself away inside True Love Books all day as a penance for the mushy, inconvenient feelings that had come over her during their chat in the courtyard the night before. They'd just spent an entire afternoon doing all the things they'd loved to do together back when they were in love, and watching him read the letters Mary and Harrison had written to each other during the war had been the icing on the cake— the very naughty, very bad-for-her cake that she had no business whatsoever eating.

But she'd dug right in anyway. Because who didn't love cake—especially when said cake was a metaphor for the first boy she'd ever kissed?

Hello?! She took a cleansing breath of rain-soaked air. *Newsflash: best not to think about kissing Sawyer while sharing an umbrella with the man.*

Too late. She was definitely thinking about it, which is precisely what she'd spent the better part of the past twelve hours doing, in spite of herself. She'd tried her best to forget about the moment when Sawyer had finished the last letter and then looked at her beloved bookshop and its glittering courtyard with the old oak tree rooting True Love so firmly in the past. It had felt like he'd finally seen the bookstore through her eyes. At last, he'd understood just what it meant to her—and while she was glad she'd been able to show that to him, the realization still left her feeling acutely vulnerable.

How did the old saying go? *Be careful what you wish for.* She'd wished she could make Sawyer understand, and once he did—once they locked back into sync with each other, the way they used to be—all the feelings she'd been bottling up for the past fifteen years had come flooding back.

Thank goodness Matt had called. Not that Jamie had any desire to speak to him—what could they possibly have to say to each other? She was thankful for the interruption, though. Who knew what would have happened if she and Sawyer had continued making eyes at one another in the moonlight?

Nothing remotely helpful for True Love Books… or for her peace of mind. That was for sure.

"So," she said, eager to keep her mind off kissing or anything remotely kissing-adjacent. Was she going to have to tattoo the words *romantic hiatus* across her forehead, so she'd see them every time she looked in the mirror? "We've talked about my past and Rick and Lucy, but I couldn't help noticing we haven't talked about *your* love life."

She was dying to know if he was seeing anyone, even casually, but up until now, she'd been afraid to ask. Truthfully, she still was. He could have fallen in love any number of times over the past fifteen years. As silly as it seemed, Jamie wasn't sure she could stomach hearing about Sawyer with another woman.

But she couldn't resist asking, romantic hiatus notwithstanding.

"Because there's not much to talk about," he said.

It was a vague response, but Jamie's heart still soared. "So no one?"

"There was a woman." He lifted his shoulder in a half shrug. He was wearing his peacoat again—the one that put her in mind of Captain Wentworth and made Jamie go all swoony. She did her best not to look at it. "Sarah. We came close."

"Close, as in...?" Jamie peered at him. Was he telling her he'd almost gotten *married?*

"I thought about proposing," he said quietly.

Jamie blinked. "Wow."

"Yeah, well. That was about the same time she met the guy who was everything she'd ever wanted. And she said it made her realize that— in her own words—we were just kind of going through the motions."

Jamie could relate. Sometimes she wondered if she'd only been going through the motions with Matt. If he'd been the love of her life, wouldn't she have wanted to move to Texas with him when he'd asked? Probably. She'd certainly been ready to pick up and move to Columbia with Sawyer. She'd even applied and been accepted.

Minor detail: Matt had asked her to come with him, and Sawyer hadn't.

Jamie cleared her throat. "Was she right?"

"Yeah...yeah!" Sawyer gave a decisive nod. "I recognized it even as she was telling me. I'd thought about proposing just because it was the time my life where I thought I should. And Sarah was—*is*, I should say—a wonderful person. But we were only ever just playing at being a couple instead of really connecting like we should."

Jamie kept her focus on the rainbow puddles on the sidewalk as they kept walking. She didn't quite trust herself to meet Sawyer's gaze when what he'd just described sounded so much like every attempt she'd made at a relationship since they'd broken up. "Are you okay?"

"Yeah. It hurt my ego, not my heart." He gave her shoulder a gentle bump with his. "I know the difference."

So did she.

The last time she'd felt truly heartbroken had been fifteen long years ago. She'd thought that meant she'd simply grown up and become more mature. But now she couldn't help wondering if she'd been holding herself back. After all, if she never fell as hard for anyone as she had for Sawyer, she'd never end up as devastated as she'd been after their break-up. But was that really a way to live?

She'd certainly thought so until Sawyer popped back into her life. She'd even been fine with the idea of taking a break from romance altogether. Now, though...

Now she wasn't so sure. About anything.

They walked the rest of the way to Jamie's house in companionable silence. It had been a while since she'd spent time with someone without feeling the need to fill the quiet moments with chatter. She'd forgotten how nice it felt to simply walk together and just *be*.

It wasn't until she paused at the walkway in front of her Cape Cod-style cottage that Sawyer seemed to realize they'd reached their destination. The rain had stopped, so he snapped the umbrella closed and finally took in the sight of the gabled roof and white picket fence.

For a second, she wondered if he'd recognize it.

Then his face broke into a broad smile. Of course he did. "You live at your parents' house?"

She nodded. "Yep. I bought it six months ago, right before they left on their big retirement trip across the continent."

They strolled toward the porch as Sawyer's gaze roamed over the house and his smile turned wistful. "Oh, yeah. They always talked about wanting to do that."

"Yep, and they did it. I just couldn't stand the thought of letting this place go."

"I'm glad you didn't." He gave their umbrella a gentle shake and water droplets flew, nourishing the pots of red begonias lining the curved walkway. "I always loved this place. Whenever I think about having a home of my own, it looks like this."

"You don't have a house?" Jamie tucked a lock of hair behind her ear to get a better look at him. She couldn't imagine grown-up Sawyer without a home of his own. He'd dreamed about buying a house for as long as she'd known him— an old, historical building that he could restore and maintain. A house with "stories in its bones," as he used to say.

"Condo, but I'm not there that much," he said.

They climbed the broad steps that lead to Jamie's front door, and the expression on Sawyer's face was so familiar that Jamie felt like she was remembering a moment they hadn't yet lived. "I thought a big house was something you always wanted."

Sawyer lingered on the threshold. "Part of being freelance means having to take jobs all over the country, wherever they are. One of the draws to Ridley is a chance to stay in one place."

Oh, right. Ridley.

For a while there, she'd forgotten all about the development company. Such a notion would have seemed impossible a few days ago.

But here...now...standing in the very spot where Sawyer had kissed her goodnight countless times before, the proposed Ridley project seemed a million miles away.

His thoughts seemed to be tracking with

hers. "How many times have I walked you to this door?" he asked in a voice as soft and tender as a memory.

Then his gaze locked onto hers, and as much as Jamie knew she should look away, she just couldn't. The lines around his eyes were new, as were the sharp angles of his jawline, but those warm brown irises of his were exactly the same. These were the eyes that had seen her at a time when no one else had. She'd been nothing but a quiet, book-loving dreamer, and he'd brought her out of her shell and shown her that the world could be every bit as colorful and vibrant in reality as it was in the novels she loved so much.

Meeting Sawyer O'Dell had changed her. He'd helped her become the woman she was today, because she'd loved the person he'd seen when he'd looked at her with those eyes—interesting, enchanting.

His.

What would it be like to feel that way again? To be loved and cherished by the only person she'd ever truly wanted to build a life with? To have her heart put back together by the man who'd broken it when he'd been just a boy?

The thought was intoxicating. It made her do things she knew she shouldn't—like step closer to him so that their breath mingled together in the evergreen air, causing her to smile to herself as his gaze drifted slowly, purposefully to her lips. Her breath hitched as he dipped his head.

She'd never wanted a kiss so badly in her life—not even when she'd been sixteen years old and he'd bent toward her in the exact same way for the very first time.

His hand was on her waist and his lips were just a whisper away—a heartbeat, a breath, a memory. And Jamie's heart felt as if it were opening like a favorite book, one whose pages hadn't been read in a long, long time. She let her eyes drift closed, because she knew this story by heart. The story of Sawyer and Jamie...

The story of us.

But in the sliver of a second before their lips met, someone said Jamie's name, and the book slammed shut.

"Jamie?"

Her eyes flew open. She and Sawyer blinked at each other, as if they couldn't quite get their bearings. Then they both turned their heads in the direction of the speaker.

No. Jamie's stomach tied itself into a knot. It couldn't be him. What on earth was he doing there?

She bit her bottom lip, still tingling from the missed opportunity. She'd been waiting fifteen years to kiss Sawyer O'Dell again, and apparently, she'd have to wait even longer.

"Matt?"

Chapter Fifteen

*J*AMIE'S HEAD SPUN. SHE FELT horribly guilty all of a sudden, like she'd just been caught doing something shameful. But she wasn't even sure whether she should feel bad for almost kissing Sawyer or for the fact that Matt had turned up so unexpectedly and spoiled the moment.

It was all so disorienting—past meets present meets past. The only thing she knew for certain was that Matt Van Horn shouldn't have been standing in her front yard. He was supposed to be in Texas, wearing a cowboy hat and pulling kids' teeth. At least that's how she'd always pictured him whenever he'd crossed her mind since he'd left—which hadn't been often, especially since Sawyer's return to Waterford.

But there he was, walking up the steps to her house with his arms spread open wide, as if she was supposed to run right into them mere seconds after she'd been on the verge of kissing another man.

She glanced back and forth between him and Sawyer. "Um...Matt. What are you...?"

"I've been trying to reach you." He stopped at the top of the stairs and cast a fleeting glance at Sawyer before aiming a wide smile in her direction. "To let you know I was coming."

What was happening? Did he really think this was some grand reunion? They hadn't even spoken in more than six months.

Which is still waaaay more recently than you and Sawyer managed before he came back.

Oh, yeah. Sawyer. He was still right there, witnessing this mortifying turn of events.

"Um, sorry." Jamie shook her head and motioned back and forth between her two exes. "Matt Van Horn, this is Sawyer O'Dell."

Sawyer extended his hand and Matt looked him up and down before shaking it. "Ah. *The* Sawyer."

"I'm sure there are others out there," Sawyer said—a valiant attempt at humor, although his smile looked more than a little strained around the edges.

His gaze lingered on Matt for a second before turning back toward Jamie and muttering under his breath. "Is this...are you all right?"

Jamie nodded. "Thanks. I'm good."

As good as a girl could be under these very bizarre and wholly confusing circumstances.

She reached for her umbrella, a clear hint for Sawyer to disappear so she could deal with Matt. "And thank you for walking me home."

And for the almost-kiss.

Although, maybe it had been fate that Matt had shown up when he did. Kissing Sawyer had never been part of the plan.

"Yeah," Sawyer said succinctly.

Then he gave Matt a curt nod and made his way down the steps without so much as a backward glance.

Jamie's stomach clenched. She tried to tell herself this was all for the best, but her inner voice wasn't very convincing.

She turned toward Matt and took a deep breath. *Focus.* But her attention darted toward Sawyer one last time to see if he was watching.

He wasn't. All she caught sight of was the back of his perfectly coifed head. So she swiveled to face Matt once again, gesturing at the door. "Do you want to come in?"

He grinned. "That'd be great."

She reached for the doorknob. "Okay."

So *not* okay. She was supposed to be kissing Sawyer right now.

Maybe...

Probably...

Definitely.

Although was kissing him right now really such a smart idea?

Obviously not. She should probably be grateful to Matt for interrupting that inappropriate moment. But for some strange reason, she could barely muster a smile for him.

So she refrained from any outward display of emotion once she'd ushered him inside the house and opted instead to fix him a cup of herbal tea. Earl Grey—it had always been Matt's favorite.

"Thanks." He warmed his hands on the steaming mug as he sat at her kitchen table, looking completely comfortable...as if he belonged there.

Did he belong there?

Jamie sat down opposite him and decided to get straight to the point. "So what are you doing here, Matt?"

He let out a little laugh. "You were always direct."

"It saves time." Time she should be spending trying to save her bookstore instead of having a tea party with her recent ex—or almost kissing her not-so-recent one. "Which I don't have a lot of right now. There's a lot going on."

Matt nodded. "I read your article in the paper about the bookstore."

"You did?" Ah, now the recent run-ins with Karen Van Horn made more sense. She'd obviously filled her son in on the recent happenings with Ridley Development. She'd probably even told Matt that Sawyer was back in town.

"The second I saw your face in the photo..." He set down his mug and sighed. "I just got hit with the biggest wave of regret. I miss you, Jamie."

This was it—the big moment she'd been dreaming about since love had walked out the door and left her behind. He was saying everything she'd longed to hear.

Except every time she'd imagined being on the receiving end of those words, they'd been coming out Sawyer's mouth. Not Matt's.

She blinked. "Just all of a sudden?"

"No, it's always been a struggle," he said, and the gleam in his dark eyes was so earnest that Jamie had to look away. Matt cleared his throat. "Are they tearing down the bookstore?"

"I don't know. I hope not." It was the million-dollar question, wasn't it? It was also the sole reason she was better off sitting across her kitchen table from Matt Van Horn than sharing an umbrella with Sawyer O'Dell.

"If it were to close..." Matt's voice drifted off and his gaze grew soft. *Here it comes.* "Would you be open to moving back to Texas with me?"

She should have been thrilled. Matt's return was the perfect fantasy of the heartbroken—the ex coming back to beg for another chance. How many times had she dreamed of Sawyer doing this exact thing after he'd left for Columbia? She'd just always thought a moment like this would make her feel happier than she did right then.

Matt pressed on. "You could come to Austin and start your own bookstore there."

Problem: Matt wasn't Sawyer.

But in a way, neither was Sawyer. He'd changed.

"Oh. Um." She shook her head. She couldn't do this. She couldn't even consider moving to Texas, not when she was still fighting for her bookshop. Just talking about re-opening True Love in Austin felt like giving up, and she wasn't ready to throw in the towel. "Matt."

"We had something, Jamie. I let that get away once. I'd be a fool not to try again." There they were again—those perfect, perfect words. "Would you think about it?"

Deep down, she knew she should tell him no. She didn't want to think about getting back together with Matt or moving clear across the country. Thinking about those things would mean giving up on True Love, and on the Waterford she'd always known and loved. And she couldn't do that...not yet.

But he'd done the one thing Sawyer had never been able to do—he'd come back and told her he'd made a mistake. That he'd like another chance with her. What more could she want?

Maybe it was time to stop living in the past and grab hold of what life had to offer. Here... now....in the present. Nothing had actually changed between her and Sawyer. He wasn't back in Waterford to stay. He was still trying to close down True Love, and she was still determined to save it.

Matt, on the other hand, had come all this way and put his heart on the line.

For true love.

For me.

He wasn't pressing for an answer, only a promise to think about what he'd just offered. She could do that. She probably *should*. Clearly, she wasn't thinking straight if she'd just nearly kissed Sawyer, so she nodded even though she felt like crying.

How could she say no?

Sawyer spent the next day forcing himself to forget about almost kissing Jamie Vaughn. He tried everything. He buried himself in work, sketching and re-sketching his designs for Ridley, even though they were pretty much perfect already. He added a tree here and there and even spent half an hour varying blades of grass from one shade of green to the next.

When that didn't take his mind off things, he took off with his messenger bag slung over his shoulder and went door to door again, schmoozing business owners. His heart wasn't in it, though. He could barely concentrate on what anyone said. He'd nod and smile and do his best to say something charming, but all the while he kept seeing Matt in his head.

Matt, of Matt & Jamie.

Matt the dentist, who was supposed to be in Texas.

Matt, who'd come charging back into town to win Jamie back.

Admittedly, Sawyer couldn't know that for sure, but he had a definite feeling. Matt just had that look about him—the confident stance, the puppy dog eyes, the overeager smile. He'd definitely been on a mission, and it didn't seem to have anything to do with flossing or brushing twice a day. The man hadn't even seemed to care that he'd stumbled upon a private moment between Sawyer and Jamie. He'd simply swooped in on his white horse and taken over.

The horse had been metaphorical, of course. And Jamie hadn't exactly seemed thrilled at his sudden reappearance. She'd seemed more stunned than anything.

But Sawyer hadn't heard a word from her all day, and that didn't bode well.

He could have called *her,* obviously. Better yet, he could have stopped by True Love while he was out and about, pounding the pavement of the business district. He very nearly did. He just wasn't sure what he could possibly say, because it was too late to tell her the things that mattered most of all.

I have feelings for you, Jamie.

I always have, and I always will.

He couldn't tell her how he felt now. If he did,

she'd think he was only doing so because he felt threatened by Matt.

Which he most definitely did.

But Matt had nothing to do with how much Jamie meant to Sawyer. Despite his best attempts at denial, he'd known he was still in love with her the minute he'd seen her standing up on that ladder in True Love. His very own Juliet, incorrect balcony references notwithstanding.

He should have told her sooner. He should have spelled it out in arugula leaves right there on the floor of Rick's Trattoria, but how could he? All she saw when she looked at him was the man who'd broken her heart, and he'd rolled back into town to do it all over again. As far as Jamie was concerned, he was the enemy of True Love...both literally and figuratively.

They'd been so close, though.

So close to reclaiming what they'd once had. So close to finding their way back to each other, despite all the complications of the Ridley project and time and distance. So close to sealing their feelings with a kiss.

And now...

Sawyer had no idea what to do.

A gentleman in his position would probably step aside and let Jamie find happiness with Matt the dentist. Sawyer couldn't promise Jamie a happy ending—in fact, a happy ending seemed all but impossible. In the end, one of them would win and the other would lose. It wasn't exactly the stuff of fairy tales.

He didn't think he could do it, though. He'd already walked away from Jamie once. How could he possibly do it again?

You won't have a choice once the Ridley project is approved.

True. And he was getting closer by the day. Shop owners had been changing their minds, one by one.

So Sawyer gritted his teeth and did his best to get through the day until Rick finally dragged him out of the house to the opening night of the Fire and Ice Festival.

Sawyer had never seen the business district so crowded before. A large banner hung over the town square welcoming people to Waterford's premier Valentine's event, and people of all ages milled about, strolling from booth to booth or pausing to enjoy street performers—fire jugglers and ice sculptors shaping huge chunks of ice into hearts or cupids. There was even a small skating rink, packed with ice skaters spinning round and round. Food vendors beneath red and white awnings sold any and all varieties of Valentine's treats: red velvet cupcakes, candy hearts, iced cookies, wine.

And chocolate everything. Sawyer's stomach growled as they passed a booth selling bourbon chocolate pound cake, but Rick didn't seem to notice.

"That must have been tough, him showing up like that," Rick said. Oh, great. They were going to talk about Matt the dentist again. "Or are we still pretending that your feelings for Jamie are platonic?"

Sawyer shook his head. He couldn't lie to his closest friend any more that he could continue lying to himself. "No. No, she's still my *kerpow*."

"Are you going to tell her that?" Rick's gaze narrowed in an over-exaggerated fashion. "Directly?"

Sawyer couldn't help but laugh. "Oh, throwing my own words back at me, I see."

Rick's dimples flashed. "It's really satisfying."

Point taken. Sawyer had somehow become equally as pathetic as Rick in the romance department. It wasn't pretty.

He rolled his shoulders and straightened his spine. They *had* to do something. "Rick, we are two smart, talented—"

"Yeah!" Rick yelled as they approached the booth for his restaurant, currently being manned by his sous chef.

"—successful men," Sawyer finished, reaching for a baguette from the tray of bread situated next to a pasta dish heating over an open flame.

"You forgot handsome." Rick gave the pasta a stir.

He was right. Rick the Romancer had the handsome part down pat, and objectively speaking, Sawyer knew he himself wasn't terrible-looking.

And yet here they were, standing on one side of the Fire and Ice Festival grounds while Jamie and Lucy worked the True Love Books booth clear on the opposite side of town square. Sawyer could still see Jamie, though, smiling at customers and handing out pink and gray envelopes. He wondered what was inside. Valentines, probably. After all, that was why the town had turned out— to celebrate the most romantic time of the year.

"Why can't we figure this out?" he asked without tearing his attention away from Jamie. The pink in her cheeks corresponded beautifully with the bright red hue of her vintage swing coat, and her blond hair whipped in the wind, swirling around her head in a golden halo.

"Oh, we figured it out." Rick followed Sawyer's gaze as he stirred. Then he shot a glance in Lucy's direction that could only be described as lovesick. "We just need to act on it."

Chapter Sixteen

*J*AMIE'S BOOTH AT THE FIRE and Ice Festival had never been so busy. She and Lucy had started passing out the copies of Mary and Harrison's correspondence as soon as the festival opened, and within an hour, word had spread.

The True Love booth had attracted a definite crowd as anxious customers, already primed by the chatter they'd overheard, couldn't wait to get their hands on the love letters. Sometimes they'd stop to unfold the pages and read them right there. Invariably, holders of the Mary letter would then try to trade it with someone for a copy of the Harrison letter and vice versa. The store was going to be packed tomorrow when Jamie made the final letter available to Valentine's shoppers. She felt giddy just thinking about it.

It was official: Mary and Harrison's letters were a hit!

Jamie beamed as she handed out more and

more pink and gray envelopes. She and Lucy kept exchanging delighted glances as their piles of letters grew smaller. Behind them, the trellis backdrop that Lucy and Rick had set up shone with twinkle lights just the like ones in the court-yard behind True Love Books. Pink blossoms from Anita's Flowers were tucked into every available nook and cranny, making their booth a fragrant explosion of color, much like a Valentine's bouquet. There were books too, of course. Piles and piles of them, from classics like *Wuthering Heights* and *Romeo and Juliet* to modern romantic comedy novels with brightly hued, animated covers. For reasons she didn't want to examine too closely, her heart gave a little squeeze every time she glanced down at the hardback copy of *Persuasion*, right at the top of the heap.

The situation with Sawyer was the absolute last thing she should be thinking about—especially now, when saving True Love suddenly didn't feel so impossible. But she and Lucy had been so busy that they'd barely had time to discuss the uncomfortable surprise meeting of Jamie's exes. Naturally, it was the first thing Lucy wanted to hear about during their first quiet moment.

"For a woman on a 'romantic hiatus,' you have a lot of guy issues," she said as Jamie passed a pink envelope to a little girl with blond braids and a pink and turquoise puffer jacket.

"Oh, I know!" Jamie was well aware of the irony of her current situation. She could have probably written a thesis on it—if she'd had the spare time lately to write anything at all, which she hadn't. "I mean, Lucy...it was like one of those fantasies where the ex shows up, groveling because they made such a huge mistake."

"I know that fantasy." Lucy pointed an envelope at her for emphasis.

"And Matt is such a good guy. Right?" She'd almost forgotten what a kind and generous person he was. There were reasons she'd dated Matt for as long as she had, even if she'd never had that fluttery, butterflies-in-her-tummy kind of feeling from him. Maybe butterflies were overrated, though. Weren't they basically just glorified moths? "You know, for so long I wondered if I just should have gone with him, but my life is here. Although, even that's up in the air now."

The town council vote on the proposed Ridley project was still slated for Valentine's Day, the day after tomorrow. True Love was running out of time.

Lucy smiled at another pair of customers, handed them each a letter, and then swiveled back toward Jamie. "What about Sawyer? Was he *super* jealous when Matt swooped in?"

"I was too numb to tell." Even thinking about the extreme awkwardness of the moment made her cringe. "Just distract me with Quentin talk, please."

"There *is* no more Quentin." Lucy sighed.

Jamie felt herself frown. "Already?"

"No spark. I'd hoped, but..." Lucy shrugged as her voice trailed off. She slipped around to the front of the booth to straighten their signage but stopped in her tracks at the sound of Rick laughing from across the crowded town square.

A line of people had formed at the booth for his restaurant, and Rick was busy scooping up plates of pasta. Once Lucy had spotted him, she couldn't seem to tear her gaze away. Jamie watched, dumbfounded, as her bestie's expression seemed to transform into an exact replica of the heart-eyes emoji.

Her mouth fell open in shock. "What was *that*?"

Lucy's face went as red as a Valentine. "What was what?"

"That look." Jamie's gaze flitted briefly to the bistro booth and back again. "At *Rick*."

"A look?" Lucy blinked. "At Rick?"

She could deny it all night long, but Jamie had seen it. Lucy looked like she'd been ready to share a single strand of spaghetti with him, *Lady and the Tramp* style. "Do you like him? And don't say 'yeah, he's my friend,' because you know what I mean."

Lucy bit her lip and stared silently for a prolonged moment, before *finally* caving and admitting the truth. "I've liked Rick since the first moment I saw him."

Jamie gasped. How had she not known that Lucy had liked Rick all along? After all those months of listening to Rick wax poetic about Lucy. All those crazy schemes of his, trying to get her to notice him...

This was unbelievable. Lucy had liked him all along! Rick was going to flip.

Should she tell Lucy that Rick was head over heels in love with her? All this secret, unrequited love stuff was just crazy. On the other hand, Rick should be the one to tell Lucy how he felt, shouldn't he?

He should. Definitely. But keeping it inside was *so* hard. Jamie clamped her hands over her mouth to keep herself from blurting out the truth.

Lucy shook her head and sighed again. "Quentin could not compare."

Jamie jumped up and down like a kid on Christmas morning. She just couldn't help it.

Lucy pointed a finger at her. "You cannot say anything!"

She couldn't be serious.

"But I want to..." Jamie flailed a hand toward Rick's booth.

"No," Lucy hissed.

This was *not* happening. How many more Valentine's Days was Jamie going to have to watch those two pine silently for one another? "It's just—"

It's just that I know he feels the same way about you!

"Uh-uh," Lucy shook her head.

"I think—"

"I said no."

"But—" Jamie was on the verge of all-out begging now.

"I said no!" Lucy hissed, then she turned to face a young woman approaching the True Love Booth. "Oh, hello. A customer."

Jamie refused to be so easily dissuaded. Lucy and Rick clearly belonged together. She knew it, Lucy knew it and Rick knew it. Fortunately, there was one other person who knew it, too.

And he just might be able to help Jamie get this romance going in time for Valentine's Day...

After helping Rick with a few things at the booth, Sawyer made his way to the Ridley coffee and hot chocolate cart. Considering this was Ridley's first appearance at the Fire and Ice Festival, he was thrilled that he'd managed to snag a decent spot, almost in the center of the town square. He and his barista passed out hot beverages and chocolate dipped strawberries while beside them, a sequins-clad twirler spun a flaming baton.

He'd be lying if he said he didn't sneak a glance at Jamie now and then, even though the idea that he might spot Matt over at the True Love Books booth made him grit his teeth. He had to do something; either step aside or make a real move. Maybe even ask Jamie out on an actual date for Valentine's Day.

Sawyer tried to formulate some kind of game plan, but he grew a little panicky when his gaze drifted over to Jamie's booth and he realized Lucy was handling things solo. Jamie was nowhere to be seen. He tried not to imagine her on a moonlight stroll somewhere with Matt while someone dressed up as Cupid shot flaming arrows over their heads. The image planted itself in his mind though, and he couldn't shake it. Not even as he supplied Beth from the hobby shop with a steady stream of caffeine and did his best to talk her into signing a contract with Ridley.

But then somewhere over Beth's shoulder, he finally spotted Jamie again, waving and trying to get his attention.

Dare he think it? *This seems promising.*

He excused himself from the discussion with Beth and made his way toward Jamie, who seemed to vibrate with intensity the closer he got. He wasn't sure whether that was good or bad, but he couldn't postpone the Matt discussion forever.

"Hey, yeah." He smiled at her. She was so beautiful in the darkness, all windswept hair and eyes lit up like sparklers.

"We have to do something," she said.

Agreed.

But what?

"About Matt?" Sawyer nodded. "I think we should just..."

Send him packing.

He couldn't say it, obviously...but he wanted to. Oh, how he wanted to...

Jamie held up a hand. "About Lucy."

"Lucy?" he echoed.

"Lucy." Jamie's upturned face split into a giddy grin. "Lucy likes Rick."

He knew it!

Thank goodness. Sawyer's days as a wingman were coming to a close. "Hallelujah! I'm going to go tell him."

He took a step toward the bistro booth, but Jamie's snagged him by his coat sleeve and reeled him back in. "No! No, you absolutely cannot tell him. I made a promise, and it would be a violation of trust."

"So." Sawyer glanced from Rick to Lucy and back at Jamie. "What do we do?"

Jamie shrugged. "Well, we have to get them together."

Obviously.

And yet...

"I thought we weren't scheming," he said.

"That was before I realized the feelings were mutual," Jamie countered.

"I'm just going to nod like that makes sense," he said, nodding.

"Valentine's Day is in two days." She threw her hands up, and Sawyer bit back a smile. When Jamie set her mind on something, there was no stopping her. Rick and Lucy would probably be engaged by the end of the night. "This whole festival is about music and romance and love and food and fun..."

Food!

Sawyer snapped his fingers. That was it.

"And food," he said. Then he repeated himself, slower, so she'd get the idea. "Fooood."

Jamie gasped, eyes dancing. "Food!"

Sawyer gave her a meaningful nod. He hoped Rick was ready—at least one of them wouldn't be spending Valentine's Day alone.

Twenty minutes later, after Jamie had told a tiny white lie in order to get Lucy to venture over to Rick's booth, she grabbed Sawyer's arm again— this time in order to pull him behind the trellis at the True Love Books & Cafe booth so they could hide and observe. She had a feeling that Rick and Lucy would be too self-conscious to admit their feelings for each other if she and Sawyer were anywhere in their field of vision. She didn't want to risk anything. It was the perfect chance for them to finally admit they were crazy about each other—Rick plus Lucy forever. No more models. No more sweater guys. Just...

Wow.

Jamie crossed her fingers, and her toes, and just about everything else that could possibly be crossed and tried to resist the crazy urge to bury her face against Sawyer's shoulder and breathe deep. He smelled like chocolate and romance—like a Valentine. Intellectually, she realized this was due to the fact that he'd been manning the Ridley cart for the past few hours, but she was having trouble thinking clearly at the moment. All the surrounding hearts and flowers at the festival were clearly getting to her.

She was supposed to be concentrating on Lucy and Rick. They needed all the positive thoughts they could get. She had a brief reprieve from Sawyer's closeness when he leaned away to peer around the edge of the latticework wall.

But then she remembered the rules and swatted his elbow. "Hey! No spying."

They'd already meddled enough, hadn't they?

"They're right out in the open," Sawyer whispered. "Rick would totally spy."

He had a point. Jamie had witnessed Rick's nosy streak on more than one occasion.

She relented, albeit a little guiltily. "Okay, a little bit of spying."

She peeked around the corner of the lattice, and Sawyer tucked himself right behind her in order to peer over her shoulder. A shiver skittered through Jamie at his nearness. He felt too good, too *right*, which was totally not the way she should feel about getting cozy with him.

But before she could move an inch, Lucy arrived at Rick's booth and it was too late.

"Hey, Jamie says you need help handing out samples." Lucy gestured toward a tray of cups filled with—what else—risotto.

Rick's eyebrows drew together. "She did?"

Behind Jamie, Sawyer groaned.

Come on, Rick. Get a clue.

"Don't you?" Lucy tilted her head, then her expression went from hopeful to disappointed. "Right," she said, shoulders sagging.

She turned to go, but Rick finally seemed to realize Jamie had sent Lucy to him for a reason.

"Wait, wait, wait." He ran around to the front of the booth to stop her. "Wait! Yes! Help. Here."

He handed her a cup of risotto, but instead of passing it on to a customer, she dug in. "So I know what I'm serving."

Rick just chuckled.

"Mmm." Lucy pointed with her spoon. "You really do make great risotto."

Rick shrugged. "I've had some practice lately."

Understatement of the century.

Lucy ate another spoonful. "How long is lately?"

Jamie held her breath and prayed that Rick understood Lucy's question. She wasn't actually talking about risotto. She'd been carrying a secret torch for Rick since the day they'd met, and she wanted to know if her feelings had been returned all along.

They had—Jamie knew how much Rick cared about Lucy. All he had to do was *tell her.*

"August ninth, two years ago," Rick said in a soft voice—so tender and gentle that Jamie almost didn't catch his words. Even if she hadn't, she would have known he'd finally confessed his feelings simply by the look on Lucy's face. Her eyes grew wide, and she looked like she was on the verge of dropping her risotto.

Rick shifted his weight from one foot to the other. "Please tell me Quentin isn't going to show up any second—"

Lucy cut him off. "He's not."

"Why not?" Rick dipped his head to meet her eyes with a questioning gaze.

Lucy swallowed. "Because he's not my *wow*."

Sawyer grabbed Jamie's hand and squeezed hard. It was happening!

"*Kerpow*," Rick said, and when Lucy's face went blank, he explained. "That's what I call it. Called it...when I first saw you."

Lucy stared at him for a long moment. Then she set her empty risotto cup aside, grabbed Rick by the lapels of his coat and hauled him toward her for a kiss.

Ahhhhh!

Jamie's gaze flew to meet Sawyer's. They looked at each other for a beat, and then...Jamie wasn't entirely sure how it happened, but the next thing she knew, she'd thrown herself into his arms. They jumped up and down in silent celebration for Lucy and Rick—at least it *started out* as a celebration. Sawyer spun Jamie around and around, and then...

Well...he didn't let go. And neither did Jamie. She couldn't seem to tear herself away from him—the soft wool of his peacoat against her cheek, the comforting strength of his arms, the exquisite beat of his heart as it crashed against hers. It was too much. Too overwhelming. Too...

Wow.

The realization hit her like Cupid's arrow, straight to her heart. Sawyer was her *wow*. And her *kerpow*. Sawyer was the one. He always had been, and he always would be.

She blinked up at him. *Oh, gosh.* What did this mean? What was she supposed to do with this information—the wholly inconvenient fact that she just might be in love with Sawyer O'Dell?

He smiled down at her, and she took a tiny backward step out of his embrace. "I need to clear up a few things," she said.

Sawyer drew in a long breath. "Matt?"

Right. Matt. Jamie needed to be honest with him once and for all, but there was also a more urgent matter at hand.

She nodded. "And the council vote is in a couple of days. And I don't know what my life is going to look like, and I just don't know if now is the right time..."

No matter how she felt about Sawyer, she still had every intention of fighting for True Love Books, and he remained the face of the opposition. That very real fact posed a serious obstacle—one that seemed far too important to overcome. Not to mention the fact that he would be packing up and moving back to Portland any day now.

This was crazy. She couldn't...*they* couldn't...

Sawyer held up a hand. "How about this—I take you to a pre-Valentine's dinner tomorrow. And we'll see where it goes from there."

A deep longing whispered through Jamie. She wanted so badly to say yes. So, *so* badly. But she also didn't want to get left behind again, especially if True Love wouldn't be there to cushion the blow.

It was just dinner, though. How much harm could come from sharing one simple meal?

And we'll see where it goes from there.

"Okay." Her throat went dry, and she had difficulty swallowing all of a sudden. She was going on a date, an actual, real date—*for Valentine's Day*—with Sawyer, her one true love and her current nemesis. What was she thinking? "Tomorrow it is."

"I'll see you at True Love." A smile tugged at Sawyer's lips, and his dark eyes went liquid in the fiery light of the festival. A girl could forgive a lot of things looking into eyes like those.

Jamie wasn't sure whether that was a good thing or a bad one.

Her heart thumped hard. "Okay."

"Okay." He nodded and lifted his hand in a wave as he backed away. "Bye."

"Bye," she said, breathless.

She stood for a moment after he'd gone, concentrating on the simple mechanics of breathing in and out and trying to imagine which would be worse—a future without True Love Books & Cafe or a future without Sawyer. Both seemed unbearable, so she tucked her hands into her pockets, pasted a smile on her face and took her place behind the counter at her booth.

The festival was drawing to close, and Mary and Harrison's love letters were nearly gone. Jamie smiled to herself as she thought about so many people in Waterford being touched by their story. As tumultuous as the past few weeks had been, there'd always been one constant—love. Whether it was romantic love, love for the community or something far simpler, like the love for books, Waterford was rich in it. The happy glow on Lucy's face when she floated back to the booth seemed to put a gigantic exclamation point on that fact.

Jamie jumped up and down and gave her a big hug. "I'm so happy for you." When they stepped apart, she winked and added, "And so relieved I don't have to listen to Rick go on and on about how amazing you are."

Lucy laughed. "Oh, no. You are still going to have to hear about that. And don't think I'm not going to ask you a million questions about how much you knew the whole time. But not now, because Rick's taking me to dinner."

Jamie clapped her hands. Love was definitely in the air. "Oh! Well, go get ready. I'll pack up."

Lucy gave Jamie another quick hug and practically skipped back toward Rick's booth. Jamie shook her head. Those two were going to make an adorable couple. She was thrilled for them, even if she still couldn't seem to figure out how to give herself the same sort of happy ending.

Case in point—Matt, whom Jamie spotted walking slowly toward her as Lucy and Rick disappeared, arm-in-arm. Her stomach tied itself into a nervous knot as she realized what she was feeling. No *wow*, no *kerpow*, just...friendly affection and slight wistfulness knowing there could never be more. He just wasn't The One, and she was pretty certain they'd both known that all along.

"Hi." She held up a hand.

"Hi," he said, but stopped short of giving her a hug or a kiss on the cheek.

Her throat tightened. She was doing the right thing. She'd made her decision even before she'd fully accepted her feelings for Sawyer, which was why she'd called Matt earlier in the day and asked him to meet her. She just hadn't been ready to share that information with anyone until she'd told Matt first. She owed him that much.

"Thank you for coming," she said.

"Thanks for calling me so soon." Matt gave her

a quiet smile. "Have you thought about what I asked?"

"I have." She nodded. "It's been buzzing around my head since I saw you."

"But, it's a 'no,'" he said, beating her to the punch.

She wasn't sure how he knew, but she had a feeling that when he really thought about it, he'd realized she wasn't his *wow* any more than he was hers. He might want her to be, but she wasn't. And that was okay.

She took his hands in hers. "Matt. I know there's a part of me that could talk myself into getting back together with you, but it wouldn't be right."

He nodded slowly, taking her words in.

"Aw, I'm sorry, Matt." She wrapped her arms around him and held him tight, much like the way she had when they'd said their goodbyes before he'd first left for Texas. But this time was different...this time, they were parting for good.

"Bye," she said as she pulled away.

"Good-bye, Jamie." He nodded again, and something about his expression told her he knew her decision was for the best.

She hoped so, anyway. But her heart still gave a tug as he walked away.

There was now one less thing standing between her and Sawyer, and even though the remaining barriers still seemed impossible to overcome, she let herself be happy for a moment.

Hopeful, even. The fourteenth was right around the corner, and she might just have a Valentine of her own this year, after all.

Chapter Seventeen

ELIOT PROWLED ALONG THE VALENTINE'S display table at True Love Books & Cafe the following afternoon, tiptoeing on his tiny ginger feet. His red heart-shaped tag dangled from his collar as he meowed at customers who stopped to pet him before selecting a letter from two baskets labeled *Harrison* and *Mary*.

Jamie smiled at her bookshop kitty. He seemed to be enjoying the huge influx of Valentine's Day shoppers as much as she and Lucy were. Before the store opened its doors earlier in the morning, a line of people had already formed outside, anxious for another installment in Mary and Harrison's saga. All day long, gasps could be heard throughout the store as readers finally learned that the lovestruck couple had been the original owners of True Love Books. It was the perfect Valentine surprise.

It was also proving to be quite good for business. By noon, they'd already topped the store's all-time record for sales in a single day, and they still had hours to go. Jamie could finally breathe a little easier. She couldn't imagine being forced to close True Love's doors—not after the way they'd been able to bring the community together over the past couple of weeks. Even better, all the new foot traffic in the store seemed to be spilling over into the other shops in the business district. The town council had to vote against Ridley tomorrow. They just had to.

It still wasn't a done deal, obviously, but Jamie felt confident enough about the fate of True Love that sometime in the afternoon, she started thinking less and less about the Ridley project and more and more about her date with Sawyer later that evening. She let herself dream and imagine what it might feel like to be Sawyer's Valentine again. Just like yesterday...

Only better.

Maybe Shakespeare had been onto something when he'd written *past is prologue*. Jamie hoped so...she hoped so with her whole heart.

She darted to the back of the store to unzip her garment bag and hang up the dress she planned on changing into before Sawyer came to escort her to dinner. The fabric was blush pink, and the dress had a full, dreamy ballerina skirt with delicate silk chiffon pleats. She planned on pairing it with tights and her favorite kitten heels. In the meantime, she still had an hour or so to go in her skinny jeans and lavender cable-knit sweater.

She pushed up her sleeves and returned to the sales floor, but her steps slowed when she spotted a familiar woman with a glossy blond bob checking out the Valentine's-themed display.

Jamie squinted. Was that Dana Sutton from Ridley?

No, it couldn't be.

What would Sawyer's boss be doing in True Love Books, lifting one of Harrison's letters from the basket and turning it over to examine the red wax seal?

Jamie glanced at Eliot, who meowed loudly, as if to confirm her suspicions. Ridley Development was right here in the building.

If ever there was a moment to face things head-on, it was now. Jamie nodded at her cat, squared her shoulders and marched right up to Dana as if she were any other customer instead of Sawyer's supervisor and all-around enemy of history and the written word.

"Ms. Sutton, right?" Jamie said, flashing a smile. After all, maybe this visit meant good news. Maybe Ridley was withdrawing its development proposal.

"Hello, Ms. Vaughn." Dana returned the unopened gray envelope in her hands to the basket.

Eliot flicked his tail and hopped down from the table.

Okay, then. Jamie would apparently be handling this conversation on her own. "Well, this is a surprise. What brings you in?"

"I thought I would stop by on my way to the festival." Dana nodded as she glanced around the bustling bookshop. "I have to say, Ms. Vaughn, generating that article was a deft move. The love letters are popular as well."

So far, so good. "Thank you."

Dana's polite smile faded. "But by now, you must realize it's a losing battle."

Jamie felt the words as if they were a physical blow to her chest. Still...the other woman couldn't be correct. Business was booming—and the effect it was bound to have on the other businesses was sure to prove that the business district could re-vitalize itself all on its own.

"Oh, no. Not at all." She gestured toward the crush of people in line for cupcakes and then at the sitting area, where an impromptu book club was poring over the latest Hallmark romance novel. "I mean, look around."

Dana's expression remained unnervingly stoic. "Yes, you're quite busy. But yours is only one store—"

"—that's bringing a lot of foot traffic into the business district." Jamie felt her own smile hard-ening into place as a terrible sense of dread bur-rowed deep in the pit of her stomach.

"For now." Dana shrugged a slender, elegant shoulder. Everything about her was perfectly polished, utterly cold. "But what about after Valentine's Day? When the lure of love goes away?"

Jamie shook her head. "Oh, the lure of love never goes away."

Of this, she was certain. Nothing was more powerful than love. It was the most universal emotion in the human experience. It transcended Valentine's Day because every day of the year, everyone wanted to be loved and to love in return— even people who tried to protect their hearts by enacting silly policies like a romantic hiatus.

Jamie knew firsthand all about that kind of secret longing. But she also knew that love was about more than romance. It was about community and family and friendship—it was even about pets. Anyone could experience love, with or without a significant other. Jamie had been heartbroken when Sawyer left for Columbia, but she'd never felt unloved. Not for a minute. She'd had her parents, Aunt Anita and her friends. She'd had True Love.

And now she had Lucy and Rick and Eliot, too. She might even have Sawyer again...

But something about Dana's presence was making that feel less and less likely.

"I suppose not." Dana glanced at the branches of the cherry tree in the center of the store, dripping with old Valentine's cards. Then she aimed a pointed look at Jamie. "But the emphasis brought on by this holiday will."

"Valentine's Day is one of the best days of the

year, and you don't have to be in a relationship to enjoy it." Jamie hoped Dana realized that. Surely she had someone in her life she could share a heart-shaped box of chocolates with—if not a boyfriend or husband, then maybe a mother, an aunt, a BFF. Possibly the stylist responsible for maintaining her hair's razor-sharp ends?

Dana nodded slowly. "But in the end, Waterford's Council is going to vote to go forward with the Ridley Property and Sawyer's redesign. He's already persuaded three more stores to support the plan, including Kagan's Bikes. Which puts us at the tipping point."

Jamie nodded—at least she thought she did. She couldn't actually tell because a cold numbness had taken over her body.

Three more businesses had signed contracts with Ridley?

She knew she shouldn't be surprised. Of course Sawyer had been working behind the scenes to build public support so he could get his re-design approved. It was his job, the entire reason he'd returned to Waterford. And it wasn't as if he'd been going about it in secret. She'd seen the coffee cart. She'd been standing with him when he'd been called over to the pizzeria. She'd even seen him schmoozing with Beth from the hobby shop last night at the festival.

The news came as a shock, all the same. And as Dana's announcement spun in her head on constant repeat, Jamie's thoughts kept snagging on the same word over and over.

He's already persuaded three more stores to support the plan...

Jamie's chest tightened, and she felt like she couldn't breathe.

Persuaded.

How had she been so stupid? Did she have to get hit in the head with a flying book to understand what had been going on the past two weeks?

"Persuade." She nodded. "Right."

She'd been thinking that Jane Austen's *Persuasion* had been a sign, some kind of magical literary promise that Sawyer might be her Captain Wentworth—that they might be destined to be together, despite all evidence to the contrary.

That book had been trying to tell her something, all right. It had been a warning sign. *Disaster approaching! Sawyer O'Dell has come to back to close your bookshop!* Any fool could have seen it.

The worst part of all was that Jamie had seen the warning signs. She'd just stopped paying attention to them somewhere along the way, choosing to believe she could have her bookstore *and* Sawyer—true love, in all its forms.

"I almost forgot that's why he's here," she said flatly.

Dana lifted her chin. "Well, that's not the real issue."

"What is?" Jamie was almost afraid of the answer.

"Your future. If...*when*...the council decides to

go ahead with the vote, and *if* you remain a hold-out, they could evoke eminent domain and take your property for the benefit of the community. Which means they'll likely pay a far lower price than what we're offering now. You have a window of opportunity, Ms. Vaughn. But it's shrinking." Dana pulled a manila envelope from her designer handbag. "This is our final offer."

The envelope practically burned Jamie's fingertips. She couldn't even look at it.

"Your store is lovely." Dana looked around again, smiling at the books and the flowers and the Valentines that decorated practically every surface. "I can see why you're fighting for it. Perhaps you can use the money from the sale to recreate it elsewhere."

"It wouldn't be the same." Jamie shook her head.

She couldn't fathom trying to build True Love again from scratch. Part of what made it so special was its history.

"I know. And I am truly sorry." Dana's expression turned bittersweet, and for the first time, Jamie got the feeling that Dana really understood what True Love meant to her.

But it was too little, too late.

The day progressed at what felt like a snail's pace for Sawyer. Somehow, he managed to get some actual work done, even though his thoughts were elsewhere entirely. While he picked up newly executed contracts at the hobby shop and Kagan's Bikes, he kept sneaking glances toward True Love Books, anxious to get business over with so he could don his red sweater and take Jamie on a proper Valentine date.

She'd said yes! He could hardly believe it. Yes, there would be challenges ahead. And yes, at tomorrow's meeting, one of them would win and the other would lose. But that was just business. Jamie was more important to him than his career. He realized that now. He'd let her go once, and he wouldn't make the same mistake again. They could make it work—somehow, some way. He knew they could.

But after he'd emailed the signed contracts to Dana and stopped by Rick's house to change into proper date night attire, he arrived at True Love Books to find the sales counter empty. In the café section, Lucy was busy firing up the espresso machine and placing pink-frosted cupcakes on antique china plates for customers, but Jamie wasn't in her usual spot at the register.

Strange.

He shot a questioning glance at Eliot, Jamie's orange tabby, but got nothing but a blithe *meow* in response. The cat then proceeded to groom his whiskers, ignoring Sawyer altogether.

Also strange.

Eliot was ordinarily extremely friendly and

social. Sawyer almost got the feeling that the cat was irritated at him for some reason, but no. That was impossible. Cats were just finicky like that sometimes, weren't they?

Even so, a flicker of worry snaked through him. Something felt off. He lingered for a moment at the Valentine's Day display on the round center table, waiting for Jamie. A heart-shaped wreath of deep red roses stood at the base of the cherry blossom tree—Anita's doing, most likely. In front of it were two baskets, one labelled *Harrison* and the other, *Mary*. A chalkboard message in a Tiffany blue frame told him to *Take One (or another)*, so he chose a silver envelope from the Harrison pile. He flicked it nervously in his hand while he scanned the area, hoping for a glimpse of Jamie.

And then he saw her, perched on the edge of one of the white Queen Anne sofas in True Love's cozy reading area. Except with her ramrod straight spine and dejected expression, she didn't appear to feel cozy at all.

Sawyer's gut tightened into a hard knot. He tucked the Harrison envelope into his pocket and strode toward her.

She looked up at him as he approached, and the sadness in her forget-me-not blue eyes just about killed him.

"What's wrong?" he said.

"Your boss, Dana Sutton, was just here." That

was when Sawyer noticed the flat manila envelope in Jamie's lap.

"Oh." He sat down beside her. "Did she say something?"

Obviously, she had. He just wished he had the benefit of knowing what it had been.

"Nothing I didn't already know." Jamie gave him a tight, humorless smile. "It was just a timely reminder."

"Of?"

"Of why you're really here. To be your charming self and persuade everyone to sell." Her voice went cold. "To persuade *me* to sell."

She stood, gripping the envelope and stomping away from him.

He flew after her. "Jamie..."

What was happening?

Surely she didn't think he'd been faking his feelings for her or that he'd asked her to dinner as some sort of bribe to accept the Ridley proposal. He wouldn't dream of acting that way, and he thought—*hoped*—Jamie knew him well enough to know better than that.

He couldn't stop dreaming about a future with her. Couldn't she see that?

"You know, I can't help but wonder." She spun around to face him, and he noticed some of the fire in her eyes had already dimmed. In its place was something worse—pain. He'd hurt her, whether he'd meant to or not. "Have you just been humoring me this whole time? Or did you ever actually give Waterford a chance?"

"My being here is all about giving Waterford a chance." That had been true from the very beginning, before he'd even known she owned True Love Books. Before he'd seen her standing atop that ladder like Juliet herself. "To help it thrive again the way I remember it used to."

The numbers didn't lie. If the town council didn't take action, the business district would crumble, one boarded-up shopfront at a time. Sawyer wouldn't be able to stand seeing that happen any more than Jamie would.

He blew out a breath. What could he possibly say to make her see what this place meant to him...what *she* meant to him? "I know you think I'm exaggerating my memories of this place to score points, but that's not true. Waterford is where the best parts of my growing up took place, where my best friends are. Where I fell in love."

Where he was falling in love again...here... now...

"In the past," she said softly. Painfully.

"'Past is prologue,' Jamie." If she wouldn't listen to him, maybe she'd listen to the bard. "I know I left when we were kids, but I'm back now and I can't stop thinking about you."

He swallowed around the sudden thickness in his throat. He'd said it—he'd told her how he felt, had been achingly honest. He just hoped he hadn't waited until it was too late.

"See, I don't know what's real and what's just you doing what you need to do to get the job so you can walk away." Her voice trembled, and her eyes shimmered with unshed tears. "Again."

Sawyer shook his head. They'd already been through this, hadn't they? "I didn't walk away. *We* agreed."

He couldn't help but think she was searching for reasons to push him away so they wouldn't have to deal with the fallout from the town council vote tomorrow. She was giving up, throwing in the towel, before they'd even had a chance.

"No." She pointed at him, and her hand trembled. "You made that decision for both of us."

He felt sick. "I never saw it like that."

"You know what? Past isn't prologue. It's *past*. Just like True Love will be soon." She gestured toward their surroundings—her beloved books, the pink tree, the handwritten Valentines tied to its branches with smooth satin ribbons. The thought of Waterford without True Love was almost inconceivable. But he'd been the one to make that call, and now he'd have to pay for that decision. "And maybe that's where we should stay, too."

No.

The price was too high. "Jamie..."

She shook her head and smiled at him, but it didn't quite reach her eyes. "No, it's okay. I'm not even mad. You're doing what you need to do, and I respect that."

He just stood there, at a complete loss. He

wanted Jamie's respect, yes. But he also wanted more. So much more.

He wanted to hold her hand and walk around the duck pond again. He wanted to take her on a picnic and let her lie down on the cool grass while he read aloud from one of her favorite novels. He wanted to kiss her in the moonlight in that beautiful courtyard beneath the branches of the old oak tree.

"I'm going to pass on dinner tonight." She took a deep breath and met his gaze, but it felt like she was looking right through him. "It was good to see you again."

Was.

They were over.

So this is it, Sawyer thought, glancing down at the envelope in her hand. He'd done what he came to Waterford to do. The town council vote would go forward, and the Ridley project would be approved. He'd won, and in the process, he'd lost the only thing that mattered.

True love.

Chapter Eighteen

SAWYER LEFT THE BOOKSHOP IN a daze, unsure where he should go or what he should do. The Valentine's dinner was off, and Rick's house wasn't exactly an option either. Rick was still walking on air, thrilled to be with Lucy after two years of unrequited love. Sawyer didn't want to rain on his parade.

So for now...

Well, for now he felt more like brooding and walking in the rain like one of the tormented heroes in the books Jamie loved so much. Heathcliff from *Wuthering Heights*, or maybe Mr. Darcy from *Pride and Prejudice*—both world-class brooders.

Sawyer bowed his head against the wind as he made his way down the cobblestone streets of the business district. For once, he had no interest in studying the architectural details of the historic buildings, so he buried his hands in the pockets of his brandy-colored leather jacket and kept his focus on the ground.

But he paused when the fingertips of his right hand made contact with something small and square. It was the envelope he'd taken from the Valentine's display at True Love Books. He'd forgotten all about it.

He turned it over to inspect the wax seal that held the envelope closed shimmery gold with the shape of a heart pressed into its center. There was no reason for him to read it. Jamie had shared the entire stack of Mary and Harrison's correspondence with him a few nights ago in the courtyard behind True Love. He wasn't sure what had possessed him to pick it up in the first place.

But he felt compelled to read it all of a sudden, as if fate had placed in his pocket for just the right moment. A ridiculous notion, but Sawyer couldn't resist slipping into a nearby coffee shop where he could sit and read it.

Like all the other storefronts in the business district, the coffee shop was all decked out for Valentine's Day. Pink and red paper chains hung from the ceiling, and the tabletops were all decorated with fragrant bouquets. Sawyer ordered a plain cup of decaf and chose a seat along the bar facing the window. A vase filled with velvety red and white long-stemmed roses loomed beside him, yet another reminder that he'd botched things with Jamie on the eve of the most romantic day of the year.

You were just doing your job, he told himself.

Sometimes he really hated his inner voice, so he chose to ignore it and instead, unfolded Harrison's letter and read the words as if he'd never seen them before.

> *My darling Mary,*
>
> *Even though we are separated by countless miles and an ocean of worry, I still feel your presence deep in my heart where I have kept you since the moment we met. As long as you continue to believe in me, believe in us, I know we can overcome any obstacle, no matter how great. Because that is the nature of true love—it always finds a way.*
>
> *Always.*

Sawyer could have written the letter himself. He felt the same way about Jamie as Harrison had about Mary. He and Jamie had been separated by more than just miles—they'd been separated by time. More than a decade. Still, he'd always held her in his heart—so deeply that he hadn't been able to have a real relationship with anyone else. He understood that now. He hadn't been able to fall in love because he was *already* in love. With Jamie.

But if their love was true, wouldn't it somehow find a way?

Could it still?

Sawyer's jaw clenched. He closed his eyes for moment and wondered if he'd been a fool to believe that he and Jamie could somehow overcome the obstacle of the Ridley project.

He wanted to believe love would find a way. He just didn't know how. But then...

He opened his eyes and lifted his gaze skyward, and he saw the tree—the beautiful old oak that Harrison and Mary had so painstakingly crafted their bookstore around—and it seemed like a sign.

If Harrison and Mary could build around the tree, couldn't he do the same? Couldn't he build something new while preserving history at the same time?

He sat for a moment, thinking about all the hours he'd put into the architectural plans for Ridley—starting over completely after his first proposal was rejected. He and Dana had spent months debating every single detail. The town council had already seen the drawings, the PowerPoint presentation and the scale model he'd spent weeks putting together. Scrapping everything now and starting over from scratch would be crazy, if not impossible. The council meeting was scheduled for tomorrow!

It just couldn't be done.

But Harrison's letter came back to him, again and again.

As long as you continue to believe in me, be-

lieve in us, *I know we can overcome any obstacle, no matter how great.*

Sawyer believed in Jamie, and he believed in their future. So he grabbed a paper napkin and a pen from his messenger bag and started sketching.

He drew for hours, barely noticing when the crowd around him grew thin. One napkin turned into two, then two into four, until he'd come up with a rough sketch of the entire business district, stitched together on coffee shop paper goods.

It could work. *Maybe.* But he was going to need to pack up and head back to Rick's house so he could have access to his laptop and electronic drawing tablet.

He drained his cup and stood, because he also needed something else—a heaping dose of caffeine. He had a long night ahead of him.

At closing time, Jamie tucked Eliot into his purple kitty carrier, locked up and headed home without a backward glance. She didn't run her fingertips over the rows of books on the shelves like she sometimes did, silently wishing them goodnight, nor did she polish the big jade leaves of the waterfall orchids like Anita had taught her to do. She didn't even pack up the pretty chiffon dress and kitten heels she'd planned on wearing out to dinner with Sawyer.

For once, she just wanted to get away—to leave True Love Books and go someplace else. Or maybe she needed practice walking away from the place she loved more than anywhere else on earth. Because like it or not, that's what she was going to have to do. She'd tried her best to save her shop, but she no longer had a choice. Come tomorrow, she was going to be forced to sign the contract with Ridley. If she didn't, she'd be left with nothing—not even enough money to rebuild.

It was nauseating. Thinking about it made her physically ill, so once she got home, she decided to skip dinner. Instead, she burrowed beneath a pile of blankets on the sofa with Eliot and her computer.

Fighting for True Love had left her little to no time for writing, but a day or two ago, she'd been struck with sudden inspiration and had started something new, something unlike anything she'd written before. She couldn't get Mary and Harrison out of her head. Their love letters were so tender, so special. How amazing would it be if she could write a romance novel based on their love story?

Eliot stretched out beside her to meticulously groom his front legs as she opened her laptop to read the notes she'd typed up when the idea for the new manuscript first struck her.

The Story of Us

Novel idea

> *Mary and Harris*
>
> *Point of view? Maybe switch between?*
>
> *Life story? Love story?*

Jamie's hands hovered over the keyboard, but she couldn't bring herself to actually type anything, even though deep in her heart she knew that this was it—this was the story she wanted to tell.

But right now, it just hurt too much. She couldn't do it, because somewhere along the way, she'd started thinking of Mary and Harrison as reflections of her and Sawyer. Reading their letters had been like looking in a mirror.

And now, she'd probably see Sawyer tomorrow for the last time—right at the moment when she lost everything that mattered most to her. This time, it was her choice to end things between them, even if it was one she'd never wanted to make. At least she hadn't simply waited around for him to leave her again. She'd made the difficult choice, the right choice to protect herself. To protect her heart.

And you ended up heartbroken anyway.

She bit the inside of her cheek to keep herself from crying. No more. The romantic hiatus was officially back on. Technically, she'd never called it off, and it wasn't as if she and Sawyer had actually gotten back together...

She blinked hard, but a lone tear managed to break free and slide down her cheek. The title at the top of her word document seemed to mock her.

The Story of Us

Could a person on a romantic hiatus even write a love story?

Doubtful—and the romantic hiatus was definitely still a thing. In fact, it might *always* be a thing. She was starting to think she was better off alone.

She reached for the delete key, ready to put the story of Harrison and Mary—and Sawyer and Jamie—behind her once and for all. That story was over. For good.

But she couldn't seem to press that button, no matter how hard she tried.

Sawyer hadn't pulled an all-nighter since college, and he'd forgotten what a toll it took on his body. His head ached, his eyes felt as if someone had poured sand directly into them, and he kept bumping into things as he changed into his best suit and packed his messenger bag. In general, he felt like garbage.

But somewhere beneath the fog in his head, hope stirred. Somehow, over the course of the past ten hours, he'd managed to completely alter the architectural plans for the Ridley project. He'd also put together a completely new animated diagram, showing the extent of the construction in detail—both old and new. He was one hundred percent ready for the town council meeting, which was scheduled to take place in the early evening.

Sawyer had a feeling the town would be pleased with what he'd come up with, even Jamie. *Especially* Jamie. He hoped so, at least. But right now, his biggest obstacle wasn't the Waterford council or the business owners or his own sleep-deprived state. It was Ridley. More specifically, Dana Sutton, who didn't have clue what Sawyer was up to.

He had to tell her, obviously. He'd need her approval in order to move forward with the new design at the council meeting. And getting that approval was going to be tricky. She'd see no reason whatsoever for reinventing the wheel when they had a solid plan currently in place and Ridley already had the majority of the town on its side. He'd have to be awfully convincing, so he didn't waste any time. He headed straight to Portland without bothering to call first, and when he burst through the doors of the Ridley offices, he found Dana sitting in the conference room with her morning cup of coffee and an untouched muffin.

She did a double take when he strode into the room. He was supposed to be in Waterford, not Portland, but they didn't have time for lengthy explanations at the moment, so he launched straight to the heart of the matter.

"There is a tree in the courtyard of True Love Books & Cafe," he said, walking directly to Dana's seat at the head of the table.

She abandoned the papers she was reading and cocked her head. "...Okay?"

Sawyer did his best to ignore the fact that she was looking at him as if he'd lost his mind. Maybe he had, but he'd managed to find his heart.

"The original builders crafted the entire store around that tree." He spread his arms out wide.

"Yeah. And probably chopped down a bunch of others in the process." Dana stood and planted a hand on her hip, a sure sign that he needed to get to the point.

"We don't know that for certain. But what we do know is that they went to extraordinary lengths to keep that tree alive and thriving."

Dana's gaze narrowed. "Where are you going with this?"

Sawyer took a deep breath. *Here goes nothing.* "I have an idea for the Waterford redesign."

"I know." She laughed. "I've seen it."

"No." He shook his head. "No, a new idea."

And for the first time since Jamie told him goodbye, he thought that maybe—just maybe—that heartbreaking conversation didn't have to be the final page of their story, after all.

This wasn't The End.

It might even be time for a new beginning.

Chapter Nineteen

*I*F THERE WAS A WORSE place than an all-romance bookstore for someone to try and power through heartbreak on Valentine's Day, it had to be a flower shop.

Jamie popped into Anita's Flowers at lunchtime, hoping for a reprieve from the lovey-dovey shoppers who'd been browsing through True Love Books & Cafe since sun-up. People were still dropping by to read Mary and Harrison's letters, but most of the customers at this point were looking for last-minute Valentine's Day presents. Jamie had been recommending romantic reads, wrapping gifts and selling poetic Valentine cards for five hours straight. She needed a break. In truth, what she really needed was a pair of bunny slippers and a pint of mint chocolate chip ice cream, but those things would have to wait until after the town council meeting. In the meantime, she needed her aunt's shoulder to cry on.

Except she hadn't anticipated being confronted by dozens upon dozens of long-stemmed red roses and festive Valentine's bouquets. She probably should have. Scratch that—she definitely should have. But she'd been so desperate for a reprieve that she'd temporarily forgotten that flowers were the number one Valentine's Day gift of choice. Fanciful arrangements covered every possible surface in her aunt's shop. The rare spaces that weren't occupied by pink and red blossoms were filled with heart-shaped balloons and giant plush animals—teddy bears dressed in red bow ties and cute white doggies holding roses in their mouths. It was kind of like getting bonked on the head by Cupid...

Or a hardback copy of *Persuasion*. Take your pick.

Fortunately, Anita had hired extra help for the day so she remained her perfectly unruffled self, the perpetual calm in the center of Jamie's storm. Anita took one look at her, then led her to a stool behind the front counter and held both her hands while Jamie poured her heart out. She told her aunt everything about the day before, from the pretty pink dress and the anticipation surrounding her dinner with Sawyer to the confrontation with Dana Sutton, and the realization that she'd let herself forget what Sawyer had come to town to do.

"I knew it. I could feel Sawyer slipping back into my heart and I should've stopped it immediately." She sliced a hand through the air, as if it would have been just that simple to cut off her emotions. In a perfect world, it would. In a perfect world, her bookstore wouldn't be in danger, either.

Anita reached to tuck a lock of Jamie's hair behind her ear and then cupped her face. Her hands smelled like roses and baby's breath—like Valentine's Day itself. "No, you shouldn't have. Never stop love. Just because you love someone and it doesn't work out doesn't mean there isn't value in the experience." She released Jamie's face and shrugged one shoulder. "Even the dentist."

"Matt," Jamie said flatly.

It would have been so easy to convince herself that Matt was the right choice for her, especially now that True Love was on the brink of closing its doors. He'd been ready to share his life with her, and he was a good man.

But he wasn't Sawyer.

"Matt." Anita nodded and gave Jamie a tender smile. "I mean, you learned something from him, didn't you?"

She had. She'd learned she wanted to hold out for her *wow* instead of settling for something that just wasn't right—but look where that decision had gotten her. "I don't want to look back. At least not with Matt. But, is that all there was between me and Sawyer? The past?"

Maybe she was just confused, lured by the

sweeping feeling of nostalgia that had come over her when he'd walked into True Love Books after so many years. He'd come back into her life in almost exactly the same spot where they'd first met, the bookshelf where *fantasy* met the *classics*. But maybe the notion that they belonged together after so much time apart *was* the fantasy.

Her throat grew thick. Falling in love with Sawyer again hadn't felt like a fantasy—it had felt real. It had felt true. But everything had gotten so complicated that she wasn't sure what to believe anymore.

"I've seen how you two look at each other *now*, and there's no doubt about how you feel." Anita's smile grew wide. "And I think it's always been there. That's how it is with true loves."

She made things sound so simple when, in fact, they were anything but. True love was about fate and destiny. It was about invisible forces bringing two people together in a way that couldn't be stopped. If what they'd found was true love then it should be easier than this, shouldn't it?

"Here I am, about to lose this bookstore that I practically grew up in—where he and I *met*—where I have put my heart and soul." She let out a shuddering breath. "All for a project that he is a part of. How can that be true love?"

Jamie shook her head and thought about the first thing Sawyer said to her when he came back to Waterford.

But, soft! What light through yonder window breaks?

He'd quoted Shakespeare. *Romeo and Juliet*, specifically. It had seemed so lovely at the time, so romantic, even with his inaccurate balcony reference. She'd been so swept off her feet by those infamous words that she'd forgotten that *Romeo and Juliet* didn't end in happily ever after. It was a tragedy.

No matter what happened with the Ridley project, there was no happy ending to be found here. Not when one of them would be in for a major disappointment. That didn't sound like a romance to Jamie, and it definitely didn't sound like true love.

But as Aunt Anita was quick to remind her, she and Sawyer weren't characters in a book. They were living, breathing people, and the real world didn't always play by literature's rules. That's what made it real instead of make-believe, fact versus fiction.

"True love doesn't have to be perfect," she said. "It just has to be true."

Just a few hours later, Jamie took a seat beside Rick, Lucy and Aunt Anita at the town council meeting. She'd moved through the remainder of the day in a daze, smiling at customers and

wrapping Valentine's Day gifts in shiny red paper, trying not to think too hard about what Anita
had said earlier.

True love didn't have to be perfect. What did
that mean, exactly? Was she supposed to pretend
that Sawyer didn't have anything to do with the
demise of her business? She wasn't sure she
could.

Even if Jamie somehow managed to close her
bookshop's doors and let herself keep falling in
love with Sawyer, there was always the chance
that one day, her grief would rear its ugly head at
some unexpected, wholly inappropriate moment.
Like maybe one day she and Sawyer would take
a fabulous vacation and just as they reached the
top of the Eiffel Tower, Jamie would turn to him
and wail, "How could you do it? How could you
make me give up True Love?"

It would be awkward to say the least. Awkward, and very much possible. Jamie was used
to wearing her heart on her sleeve, not repressing
her feelings. She'd always considered that to be a
good thing, but now she wasn't so sure.

No, she decided the second Sawyer walked
into the room and took his place next to Dana
beside the lectern. *It's definitely a bad thing.* Her
face went instantly hot, and she was certain every person within a five-mile radius could tell she
was hopelessly in love with Sawyer O'Dell.

Emphasis on *hopeless.*

She forced herself to look away, focusing

instead on the crowd assembled for the meeting. Every single shopkeeper from the business district was in attendance—Olga from the dance studio, Beth from the hobby shop, Chuck from the pizzeria, along with his dad. So many others, too. A long conference table had been set up along one of the side walls, where members of the town council sat facing forward. Eric was situated right in the center with a gavel in his hand and a microphone stand in front of him.

Everything looked so official. It was impossible not to feel at least a little bit intimidated. Before she could stop herself, Jamie glanced at Sawyer in search of comfort. Big mistake, obviously. Huge. His warm brown eyes looked as soft as velvet and as soon as their gazes locked, Jamie found it impossible to look away.

True love doesn't have to be perfect. It just has to be true.

Her heart beat impossibly hard.

"Whenever you're ready," Eric said into the microphone, prompting Dana to step up to the lectern and begin the presentation.

"Thank you. Council members, I'm Dana Sutton. With me is Sawyer O'Dell, and together we represent Ridley Property Development..." As if Jamie needed the reminder. She felt Lucy's gaze on her, checking to make sure she was okay, but she kept her focus straight ahead as Dana continued, "...which, as you know, has presented a proposal for a redesign to the Waterford Business District."

Gosh, this was painful.

Jamie squirmed in her chair, almost wishing they would just commence with the vote and call it a day. She didn't have the emotional bandwidth for another splashy presentation of the architectural renderings of her beloved business district disappearing to make way for some hideous spaceship, and she was pretty certain that was what was next on the agenda because a drop-down screen began to unfurl behind Sawyer's head.

Dana dazzled at the lectern. "We are here today to withdraw that proposal."

Wait.

What?

The room buzzed with interest. Lucy grabbed Jamie's arm, and she knew she should probably react. But she couldn't. Until she knew exactly what was going on, all she could do was sit there numbly, afraid to get her hopes up.

But then Sawyer shot her a tiny, almost imperceptible wink...and her spirits rose like a buoyant, beautiful, heart-shaped balloon on a string.

"And we'd like to present a new one." Dana turned toward Eric and his colleagues. "If the council is amenable."

Eric leaned forward in his chair. "You realize this will mean we'll have to delay the vote until everyone has a chance to review the designs, in depth?"

"We do. And, honestly? My business instincts are completely against this." Dana pressed a hand to her heart, and Jamie was more bemused than ever. "But my creative instinct says that what Sawyer came up with deserves to be seen."

Eric nodded. "Well, then, let's see it."

Dana stepped aside to make room for Sawyer at the lectern as the lights dimmed.

He looked out over the audience, briefly locking eyes with Jamie again before he spoke. "Everybody wants the Waterford business district to succeed. The question is—which direction do we take in order to achieve that goal?"

He pointed a clicker toward a projector set up on a small table beside the podium, and a current image of the Waterford business district flashed onto the screen. "If we only choose to preserve history, then we risk failing to revitalize the business district and losing out on the opportunity to bring new business to Waterford."

He clicked again, and the onscreen image switched to the three-dimensional design that Ridley presented at the previous town council meeting.

"If we just wipe the slate clean, we lose the charm and history of what makes Waterford the kind of place we like to call home," he said. Then he took a deep breath and aimed a quiet smile directly at Jamie. "But after being back here for the first time in a long time, and having several conversations with the very persuasive Ms. Jamie Vaughn..."

His eyes twinkled, and Jamie couldn't move, couldn't even breathe.

"...I started thinking about another route," he said. This time, when he pressed the clicker, a new version of the design appeared.

Sawyer's drawings came alive, spinning and revealing themselves, piece by piece. The plans definitely included a new building, but on the ground floor, supporting the new construction, the town favorites remained—the pizzeria, Anita's Flowers, Olga's Dance Studio, Beth's Hobby World, Kagan's Bikes. He'd even including the duck crossings.

And at the glorious center of everything stood True Love Books & Cafe on its original street corner with the old oak tree towering over its courtyard. Jamie couldn't believe it. It was everything she wanted—and more, because even though the existing shops were still part of the new project in the same storefronts they currently occupied, the presentation included many charming improvements. Doggy water fountains were evenly spaced along the sidewalk, a huge pergola was placed over the entrance to Anita's Flowers as a support for the elaborate flower arches she'd always wanted to create, and the pizzeria now had a wide picture window where passers-by could stop and watch pizza dough being tossed into the air.

The Ridley coffee cart was still a thing too, parked at a jaunty angle near the entrance to the park, with a pretty striped awning, barstools and a sign promising free hot chocolate on snowy days.

Jamie glanced at a beaming Anita, then at Rick and Lucy, who exchanged a definite *I knew it* look. So this was real...she hadn't imagined it. Sawyer had listened to her. He'd truly paid attention to all the things she'd been telling him about Waterford and True Love and the old oak tree. Even better, he'd come to understand what made their town so special, because all the added touches were beyond her wildest dreams. So sweet, so perfectly Waterford.

Her breath hitched. All this time she'd been doubting him, when in fact, Sawyer really was a true hometown boy.

True.

She blinked back tears as he finished his presentation.

"I believe this new design will help foster the sense of Waterford's history and community while respecting the past, honoring the present..." He paused, cleared his throat, and his final words seemed to carry a tender promise. "...and planning for the future."

"Thank you, Mr. O'Dell. Now..." Eric picked up his gavel, and before she could stop herself, Jamie flew to her feet.

"Can I say something?" she blurted.

Teri Wilson

Every head in the room turned in her direction. Most notably, Sawyer's.

Eric nodded. "Please, Ms. Vaughn."

She walked slowly to the podium, and both Sawyer and Dana stepped aside to give her some space at the lectern. She wanted to get this right—*needed* to get it right. There were so many emotions tumbling around inside her, she didn't quite trust herself to speak without breaking down.

But she had to. Sawyer had done the impossible. He'd paved a way toward a future...for both of them and for Waterford. There was no way she could let the meeting adjourn until she let the council, and the town itself, know how she felt.

"Hi. As most of you know, I have been leading the opposition to the redesign. To me, there is a magic to the history of this place." She held her arms out, encompassing everyone in the room. "In the story of us."

A muscle in Sawyer's jaw visibly tensed, and Jamie realized he was nervous.

So she fixed her gaze with his and said, "However, that doesn't mean we have to sacrifice our future. And after looking at Mr. O'Dell's *new* designs, I believe he's found a way to bridge the divide. For which I am profoundly grateful."

Her voice broke, and something inside her broke along with it. She was so tired of fighting... All this time, she'd thought she had been fighting for True Love, and in a way she had been, but she'd also been fighting against it—against the feelings she had for Sawyer, her one true love. She couldn't do it anymore. She was ready to concede.

Her heart raced, and this time, when butterflies took flight in her tummy, she welcomed them. "So for what it's worth, the *re*design from Ridley has my full support."

Everyone clapped. Someone let out a loud whoop, which Jamie suspected came from Rick.

"Clearly, your support is worth a great deal, Ms. Vaughn," Eric said, picking up his gavel again. "If there are no objections, we would like to table the discussion until next week. But, as for me, I agree with Ms. Vaughn. I like it."

The gavel came down, and just like that, true love won.

The second Eric banged his gavel, Sawyer was swept up in a wave of congratulations and effusive gratitude. Beth insisted on taking half a dozen selfies with him so she could scrapbook the moment at the next craft class at her hobby store. Chuck and his father said they wanted him to be the first person to toss a pizza up in the air in the special window display. Olga even promised him free ballet lessons. At long last, all of Waterford welcomed him back with open arms.

It felt good—better than he ever could have imagined. He wanted to stay and soak it all up, but he couldn't help craning his neck and peering over heads in search of Jamie. They needed to talk, obviously. She'd thrown her public support behind the proposal, and he was pretty sure she might be willing to go on that Valentine's dinner date with him now, but she was nowhere to be seen. She seemed to have vanished into thin air once the meeting had adjourned.

He tried to not panic. He'd find her. He'd search every square inch of Waterford looking for her if he had to, but there was still one more very important detail to be settled first.

He felt a hand land on his shoulder as he wrapped up a conversation with a few members of the town council and turned to find Dana waiting to speak with him. Good. He wouldn't be able to face Jamie until he got this out of the way.

"Sawyer, congratulations. I feel confident that we'll be welcoming you to Ridley Properties very soon," she said.

They were the words Sawyer had been waiting to hear for months. *Years*, actually. A permanent job at Ridley would give him the security and stability he'd been searching for all his adult life. No more living out of a suitcase, no more moving from one town to the next every few years as he'd done when he'd been a child. Living in Portland full-time was everything he'd wanted.

But now he wanted something different, something more.

"Thank you, Dana. Thank you for everything, especially all your support tonight." He'd been sort of stunned when she'd agreed to present the revised plan, especially on such short notice—which made rejecting a job at Ridley all the more difficult. "But..."

Her eyebrows rose. "*But?*"

In all the time Sawyer had known Dana, she'd always seemed entirely calm and collected. Nothing and no one caught her by surprise, but apparently, he just had. She blinked slowly at him as if waiting for him to tell her he'd misspoken.

He took a deep breath and did his best to explain. "You said that one of the things you liked about my work was my ability to anticipate the client's needs."

She pasted on a smile. "Which you just demonstrated."

"But I think that it's time for me to listen to my own needs. And I need to make *a home*, a real home." He wanted it all—the house, the white picket fence—and Jamie Vaughn...*if* she would have him. Either way, this was where he belonged. It always had been, and it always would be. "And I would like it to be in Waterford."

Dana let out a huge breath and shook her head, visibly relieved. "And you think that prevents you from working at Ridley?"

He narrowed his gaze at her. "Doesn't it?"

"Sawyer, you just pulled off a tremendous success that goes far beyond your talent for architecture. I'm not letting you go that easily. You want to be in Waterford?" She waved a hand at the people still milling about the town hall. *His* people. *His* town. "Fine."

Sawyer didn't know what to say. He just stared at her, dumbfounded. He'd been ready to give up everything to build a life in Waterford... to stay. And now Dana was telling him he might not have to give up anything at all. It seemed too good to be true.

"You have to be here while the project goes forward, anyway. Afterward, we'll renegotiate. And I anticipate that it will go very well." She gave him a rare, broad smile. Coming from Dana, it was all the assurance he needed. "For both of us."

Then she patted his shoulder and walked away, finally leaving him free to find Jamie—except he still couldn't catch a glimpse of her angelic smile or her halo of blond waves anywhere. He thought for certain she'd be busy chatting with her aunt or Lucy and Rick, who'd been making googly eyes at each other for two days straight, but the three of them stood off to the side together, watching him in a way that gave him pause.

He tucked his hands into the pockets of his suit jacket and strolled over to them, taking the bait. "Where's Jamie?"

Anita gave a little shrug. "She's not here."

"Okay." Sawyer glanced from one of them to the next. They looked like three identical cats who'd swallowed the canaries. "Where is she?"

"She told me to give you this." Lucy pulled something from her pocket and handed it to him. A red envelope with his name written on it in Jamie's swirling, romantic script.

He took it, tracing the distinctive handwriting with the pad of his thumb. It looked like something from Jane Austen's day. So perfectly literary; so perfectly Jamie. "What's this?"

"It's a red envelope on Valentine's Day. It's a Valentine," Rick said, because apparently he was an expert on romance now that he'd gotten his girl.

Sawyer laughed, shook his head and opened the envelope. It contained a square card— vintage, of course—with a single letter written in the corner. J for Jamie. He turned it over in his hands, wondering what he might be missing, but then he realized the envelope still felt weighted down by something else inside.

He turned it over, and a flash of silver fell into his palm. A single, shiny key on a sterling heart-shaped keyring. Fresh energy filled him. He felt light on his feet all of a sudden, as if maybe Olga could actually turn him into Prince Charming on the ballet stage. The key in his hand wasn't just any key...

Jamie had given him the key to True Love, the one and only key to her heart.

He closed his fist around it, holding it tight.

Rick winked at him.

And as Sawyer all but sprinted for the door, Anita called out, "Have fun."

He ran all the way to the bookstore, his wingtip shoes pounding the cobblestones for the entire three blocks. The moon shone high overhead, casting a soft glow over Waterford, as pink as a bouquet of cotton candy carnations—a Valentine's moon, a moon for sweethearts. The old oak's branches swayed as if the tree were dancing to some invisible music, and Sawyer was so hopeful, he could practically hear it. It was lilting and lovely and reminded him of the song he and Jamie had danced to at their senior prom.

That night seemed so far away now, and at the same time, it felt like yesterday. He could still remember the scent of Jamie's bluebell perfume and how soft and delicate her tulle princess dress had felt against his palm when he slid his hand onto the small of her back. He'd felt invincible then, so full of dreams and plans for the future. How had it taken him so long to find that feeling again?

It no longer mattered. He was here now, for good. His pulse roared in his ears, and he squeezed the silver keyring so hard that when he reached the threshold of True Love Books and unclenched his fist, the shape of a heart had pressed itself into his flesh.

He stood at the door, breathless in the cold of

a pine-scented, Pacific Northwest night. The windows of the shop were darkened, but flickering shadows of candlelight waltzed across the shelves of books. As he reached to slide the key into the door's lock, he spotted Eliot in the front window, watching him with his fat orange tail wrapped contently around his paws.

The door creaked open, and Sawyer stepped inside, heart still thumping wildly in his chest. But the sight that greeted him caused him to grow still. Reverent. It was the same True Love he'd known since he was a boy—of course it was. But now a path had been laid out for him—a trail of red rose petals, flanked on either side by luminous votive candles.

So this was why Jamie had disappeared so quickly after the town council meeting. He smiled to himself and walked gingerly over the rose petals as the trail wound through the branches of the cherry tree dripping with ribbons and Valentines, past the corner where the classics met fantasy, toward the blooming pink flower wall and the French doors leading to the courtyard.

A light fog had blown in from the coast, giving the courtyard a dreamy, ethereal feeling as he made his way toward the café table closest to the fountain. It was the same table where he'd sat just a few nights ago, reading the letters Mary and Harrison had exchanged while they'd been apart. Now a gourmet spread was laid out on the table—the Valentine's dinner they'd promised to share. Jamie must have gotten a little help from Rick, which seemed only fair after all they'd done to help Rick and Lucy finally get together. Sawyer let out soft laugh. It hung in the air as vapor as he picked up the hardback volume that had been placed next to his plate.

The Princess Bride.

Naturally. Sawyer shook his head in wonder. The book's worn spine and gently loved cover hinted it might be the exact same copy he and Jamie had both tried to nab on the day they'd met. She'd kept it, all these years.

"So I started writing something new." Jamie's voice reached him from somewhere behind him as he flipped through the book's soft pages.

He turned around, and there she was, bathed in the pale glow of fairy lights and a sweetheart moon. She wore a pink dress with a pleated ballerina skirt that looked as light as air, and the love in her eyes as she looked at him nearly brought him to his knees.

"A love story." She came a few steps closer. "And I would like your opinion on it."

His throat grew thick with emotion, but somehow, he managed to form a few words. "What's it about?"

"Well, a girl and boy meet. Fall in love. Then they get separated, only for circumstances to bring them back together again." She closed the remaining distance between them and laid her dainty hand over his heart. "And they realize they never stopped loving each other the entire time. And that's how you know it's true love."

He reached for her hand, still resting on his chest, and covered it with his. "That's my favorite kind of story."

"Mine too." She took a deep breath and gave him a tentative smile. "But I'm going to need your help to finish it."

It was her way of asking him if he was back in Waterford to stay this time. He knew this as surely as he knew his own name.

The answer burned deep within him, warming his soul. "And you will have it."

He cupped her face in his hands and ran the pad of his thumb over her trembling bottom lip. She gazed up at him through a veil of unshed tears, and it felt as if they were truly seeing each other for the first time.

His Jamie.

His home.

His one true love.

"Always," he whispered.

Then, at long last, an adult Sawyer O'Dell kissed a grown-up Jamie Vaughn, and the moment their lips met, the years they'd spent apart seemed to melt away.

It was a kiss steeped in fairy tales and history and faded Valentines written long ago. A kiss born of literature and love stories, but better because it was real...true.

And somewhere beneath the pounding of his

heart, Sawyer could have sworn he heard fate whispering in his ear, like the narrator of a story.

And they lived happily ever after.

Epilogue

One year later...

*T*HE ONLY WAY VALENTINE'S DAY could possibly top the previous year was if the grand re-opening of the Waterford business district happened to fall on February 14, which also happened to be the same exact day as the launch party for Jamie's first published novel, *The Story of Us*. By some miracle, all three events perfectly coincided—the book launch, the unveiling of the newly restored business district and Valentine's Day, which had long been Jamie's favorite holiday. This year it carried special meaning, of course, because it also marked the one-year anniversary of Sawyer's official, permanent homecoming.

So much had happened since that night he'd kissed her in the courtyard of True Love Books & Cafe. Sawyer had purchased a little cottage, just one street over from the house she'd bought from her parents. He'd celebrated the occasion with a housewarming party—catered by Rick, naturally—that had included a backyard bonfire where he'd set his suitcase aflame. The following morning, he'd broken ground on the Ridley project, and life for both of them had been a whirlwind ever since.

Jamie had been forced to close True Love Books, but only temporarily while the block was under construction. The timing was most convenient, because only a month prior, she'd sold her manuscript to a publisher—a longstanding publishing company in New York City that had put out books she'd adored since childhood. When the call came, she'd had to pinch herself, because the good news had felt more like a dream than real life. Then she'd been buried in line edits and copyedits and proofreading, and the temporary closure of her bookshop had felt like a blessing in disguise.

She couldn't wait to open back up again, though. She missed spending her days working side-by-side with Lucy, who'd recently begun rocking a glittering diamond ring on a very important finger. She missed being surrounded by the scents of ink on paper, crystal bowls filled with Anita's flowers and the sweet aroma of Rick's buttercream cupcakes in the café. Mostly, she missed the feeling she'd always gotten that True Love was a very real part of the glue that held the community together—the beautiful beating heart of Waterford.

She hoped it wasn't weird that the front display table would be piled high with copies of her very own novel for the grand reopening. She couldn't resist, because in addition to being a love story about two lost soulmates finding their way back to each other, her book was also a tribute to the community. Beyond the romance and the poetic language, she'd written a love letter to Waterford itself, setting her story on the very streets where Mary and Harrison had walked so long ago and where she and Sawyer had fallen in love.

Twice.

She had a sneaking suspicion that the unveiling of the Ridley enterprise falling on Valentine's Day was more than just a coincidence. After all, Sawyer had acted as the lead architect on the project, so the scheduled completion date had definitely been his doing. He was also well aware that Jamie's book was scheduled to be released that day, "the most romantic day of the year" according to her editor. But restructuring the landscape of a town as old as Waterford hadn't exactly been an easy task. There had been plenty of surprises along the way, including rusted-out pipes, foundations requiring extensive repair, and permits necessitating the approval of the state's historical preservation office. Sawyer had navigated it all like a pro, even surprising Jamie with a brand-new plaque for True Love's front door, proclaiming the bookshop an official Oregon State Historical Landmark.

Never again would she have to worry about True Love Books & Cafe closing its doors. It was a permanent part of Waterford's story now—past, present and future.

"I still can't believe you did this," she said, polishing the gilded border of the plaque as Sawyer approached.

Instead of his ever-present messenger bag, Eliot's purple cat carrier swung from his shoulder. Since Jamie had been up with the dawn getting the store ready for her book party, he'd volunteered to stop by Jamie's house to feed the kitty breakfast at his preferred wake-up time and then bring the furry beast to True Love in time for the action. Eliot and Sawyer had become as thick as thieves in the past few months. In fact, as of Christmas morning, Sawyer had become the proud owner of a coffee mug that said *Cat Dad*... much to Rick's amusement.

Sawyer gave Jamie a gentle kiss when he reached the threshold of the store, and then tilted his head. "Can't believe I did what?"

She'd been talking about the plaque—and the store's designation as a landmark—but looking at him standing there in the center of the business district that he'd worked so hard to save, she realized she meant something else. Something bigger.

"All of this," she said, her voice dropping to

aching whisper. "Waterford owes you so much. So do I."

"Hey, now. You don't owe me a thing." He reached for her hand, lifted it to his lips and covered it with a tender kiss. "I adore you. You know that, but can we go inside? Your cat has gotten significantly heavier recently. Someone must be feeding him too many treats."

Jamie rolled her eyes as she pushed the door open. "Gee, I wonder who that could be."

"No idea," Sawyer deadpanned as he deposited the cat carrier on the countertop by the register.

"Seriously, Hometown Boy." It had become a term of endearment that Jamie had no intention of retiring anytime soon. "You've set a new bar for Valentine's Day. This day couldn't possibly get any better."

She unzipped Eliot's carrier, and he popped out of the opening in a flurry of ginger fur and an unmistakable flash of sparkle.

"You sure about that?" Sawyer murmured, brushing Jamie's hair aside to press his lips to the curve of her neck.

It was then that Jamie saw it—the source of the glittering light coming from Eliot's collar. Alongside his heart-shaped pet tag, an antique engagement ring had been tied to his collar with pink satin ribbon, the same kind she'd used to affix the old Valentines from The *Story of Us* box to True Love's cherry tree for the second year in a row, a tradition in the making.

She gasped, not quite believing what she was seeing.

"I searched high and low for a ring that matched the one Harrison gave to Mary after he came back from the war. Remember, from the picture of Mary you found in the attic when we were getting ready for the renovation?" Sawyer said in a voice raw with emotion as he untied the ribbon from around Eliot's collar.

Of course she remembered. She'd just never imagined Sawyer would one day slip a similar ring on her finger.

She nodded, too afraid to speak lest she start crying and spoil the moment. Then Sawyer dropped down on one knee and before he could say another word, a loud, resounding *"Yes!"* came flying out of her mouth.

He laughed and slid the vintage ring onto her finger. Jamie was pretty sure he officially popped the question, but she couldn't make out the words because she was crying in earnest now. And she didn't care, because she realized there was no spoiling a moment like this one. It had been over a decade and a half in the making.

Jamie brushed the tears from her face and threw herself into Sawyer's arms, and he held her onto her so tightly that it felt like he'd never let go. Eliot meowed loudly, rubbing against their entwined legs, and somewhere over Sawyer's shoulder, Jamie caught sight of *Persuasion* by Jane Austen, lined up neatly on the top shelf.

Jamie's favorite lines from the novel wove their way into her thoughts, just as they had on the day she'd nearly dropped the very same book on Sawyer's head.

You pierce my soul. I am half agony, half hope. Tell me that I am not too late...

She squeezed her eyes shut and pressed her face into the solid warmth of Sawyer's chest.

You're not too late, my love. You're right on time.

The End

Wild Mushroom and Asparagus Risotto

A Hallmark Original Recipe

In *The Story of Us*, Jamie and Sawyer's friend Rick can't seem to tell his crush how he feels about her. More than once, he retreats to the kitchen to make risotto instead. Jamie and Sawyer aren't especially good at putting their feelings for each other into words, either...and it doesn't help that Sawyer's retail development plan will mean the end of Jamie's beloved bookstore! Our Wild Mushroom and Asparagus Risotto is as easy as it is elegant. It would be perfect to serve to friends or as part of a romantic meal.

Yield: 6 servings
Prep Time: 15 minutes
Cook Time: 45 minutes
Total Time: 1 hour

INGREDIENTS

- 4 tablespoons butter, divided
- 8 ounces wild mushroom blend (such as cremini, portobello, shitake), trimmed, sliced
- 1 pound asparagus, trimmed, cut into 1-inch pieces
- 6 cups chicken broth
- 2 tablespoons olive oil
- 1 small yellow onion, finely chopped
- 1 garlic clove, minced
- 1½ cups arborio rice
- 1 cup dry white wine
- ½ cup grated Parmesan cheese
- ½ teaspoon grated nutmeg
- Kosher salt and black pepper, as needed
- 2 tablespoons shaved Parmesan
- Fresh Italian parsley, as needed

DIRECTIONS

1. Heat 2 tablespoons butter in a sauté pan; add mushrooms and cook over medium heat until all moisture has evaporated and mushrooms are golden brown. Season to taste with salt and black pepper and set aside.

2. Heat 1 tablespoon butter in a sauté pan; add asparagus and cook over medium-low heat for 3 to 5 minutes or until tender. Season to taste with salt and black pepper and set aside.
3. In a saucepan, heat chicken broth to a low simmer. Keep warm.
4. Heat olive oil in a heavy 4-quart saucepan; add onions and garlic; cook over low heat for 5 minutes, or until translucent. Add arborio rice and cook for 3 minutes or until grains are evenly coated and translucent around outer edges, stirring frequently. Reduce heat to low. Add white wine and cook for about 1 minute, stirring constantly, until all liquid is absorbed.
5. Ladle 1 cup hot chicken broth over rice and stir until liquid is absorbed. Continue adding broth, one ladle at a time, stirring frequently, until rice is tender yet firm to the bite and has a creamy appearance, about 20 to 25 minutes. Remove from heat.
6. Add grated Parmesan, nutmeg, remaining butter, reserved asparagus and mushrooms; gently toss to blend. Taste and adjust seasoning, if needed.
7. Serve risotto immediately garnished with shaved Parmesan and parsley.

Thanks so much for reading *The Story of Us*. We hope you enjoyed it!

You might like these other books from Hallmark Publishing:

Love at the Shore
Country Hearts
Love By Chance
Love Locks
A Dash of Love
Love on Location
Beach Wedding Weekend
Sunrise Cabin

For information about our new releases and exclusive offers, sign up for our free newsletter at hallmarkchannel.com/hallmark-publishing-newsletter

You can also connect with us here:

Facebook.com/HallmarkPublishing

Twitter.com/HallmarkPublish

About the Author

Teri Wilson is the Publishers Weekly bestselling author/creator of the Hallmark Channel Original Movies *Unleashing Mr. Darcy, Marrying Mr. Darcy, The Art of Us,* and *Northern Lights of Christmas,* based on her book *Sleigh Bell Sweethearts*. She is also a recipient of the prestigious RITA Award for excellence in romantic fiction. Teri has a major weakness for cute animals, pretty dresses and Audrey Hepburn films, and she loves following the British royal family. Visit her at www.teriwilson.net or on Twitter @TeriWilsonauthr.

Turn the page for a sneak peek of

CINDI
MADSEN

COUNTRY
HEARTS

CHAPTER ONE

T*his is what I get for saying I wanted an adventure.*

"Wanted" sounded much better than "no other
alternatives."

When whisperings of budget cuts became a
reality, the principal of the school Jemma had
worked at for three years had called her into his
office. He told her that the administration was
sorry, but they had to lay her off. Considering her
limited options, she'd had to smother her panic,
roll with the punches, and take a risk.

As she sat in the living room of the cottage
she'd been renting for all of a day, she experienced a pinch of loneliness. Add her worries
about the raging storm outside, and she struggled to maintain the optimism she'd kept a tight
grip on since taking the temporary teaching position. In a tiny Colorado town she'd never heard of
before finding the job posting, no less.

The truth was, she did need something new. A bit of a shakeup to get her out of her funk. While she could handle a classroom full of kids like nobody's business—partially because she understood occasionally losing focus and the importance of making learning fun—she was working on taking control and being less of a hot mess in her personal life. On being bolder and having the courage to meet new people and take more chances.

Surely seizing the opportunity to live somewhere besides the city where she'd grown up would help with that, even if it was a forced sort of help.

A crack of thunder vibrated the window panes, and a little shriek escaped. Since she'd nearly spilled her tea, Jemma set her favorite extra-large mug on the coffee table and tightened her fuzzy fleece blanket around herself. *It's an adventure. It's an adventure.*

When people said they wanted an adventure, usually exotic locations or rollercoasters came to mind. Bungee jumping. That kind of thing. Whereas she shuddered at the idea of trusting a rickety man-made machine or flinging herself off a bridge. What if something went wrong? Did people really trust a cord to catch them? Because she certainly didn't.

It wasn't that she was the type of person to need her entire life mapped out or for everything to go according to plan. No, as a third-grade teacher, she'd forever be disappointed if she let curve balls get to her. If there was one thing you couldn't plan for, it was what would pop out of a kid's mouth next. But she needed to be more organized and less idealistic, and the next time she was in a relationship, she wouldn't be the only one aware it was happening.

How could I have been so clueless? Why didn't I confirm we were dating instead of hanging out?

It definitely would've saved her a lot of frustration and sorrow. It made her feel delusional to mourn the loss of a boyfriend who'd turned out to only be a friend. Especially since in the beginning, she'd passed up a more-secure position to stay at the school where Simon worked so they could grow that friendship into more.

Maybe I should just give up on guys altogether and embrace the idea of being single forever.

The wind outside picked up speed, rattling the shutters on the window, and her heart rate kicked up a few notches. She glanced at the large black-and-white bunny at her side. "You'll protect me, won't you, Señor Fluffypants?"

Her former students had helped her name him, settling on Señor Fluffypants because of the black patch of fur over his nose that looked like a moustache. She'd had him since he could fit in her palm, but he'd grown into a four-pound snuggly floofball.

At the next grumbling burp of thunder, he jumped off the cushion next to her and rushed under the couch. So much for her knight in fluffy armor.

No need to be scared. Surely this house would've blown away long ago if it was that fragile.

Or maybe the years of decay will catch up now that I've decided to move in.

With its cheery blue trim and shutters, and the faint remains of vines crawling across the white exterior, the country cottage had looked so idyllic. Likc shc could spcnd hcr weekends curled up on the couch with her tea and a book and get lost for a few hours.

Now she felt lost in the way that she didn't know anyone, her bunny had abandoned her, and she couldn't concentrate on her book with the storm raging outside. Who knew thunder could be that loud?

The sky lit up outside, a streak of lightning making the world bright before it went dark again.

Man, I wish I could call up Randa and beg her to come over. Her fellow teacher had started out as Jemma's mentor, but they'd quickly become best friends. When Jemma had freaked out over being fired and asked how on earth she was supposed to pay her student loans and bills, Randa had talked her down from the ledge. She'd reminded Jemma of all the times they'd tried new activities—like the time Randa had convinced her to eat at the new Indian food restaurant and Jemma had found a new spicy dish to love, tingling lips and all. Or how they'd accidentally made a wrong turn and ended up completely lost but laughing until they were crying.

They called their mishaps adventures, and because of those adventures, they'd tried out more interesting restaurants and had funny stories to tell in the teachers' lounge and at parties.

With that in mind, Jemma had pulled up her bootstraps and cast a wide net as she'd searched for a new position. Even with good references and Randa's connections, no one was hiring— not mid-year, when most contracts were already filled.

But then Jemma had found a listing to cover for a third-grade teacher on maternity leave. She'd applied on a whim, and when Principal Alvarez had called for an interview and they'd hit it off, Jemma had become convinced this was the position for her.

And when she'd experienced a bit of trepidation over moving to the small town of Haven Lake where she didn't know anyone, she'd told herself it'd been a while since she'd had a real adventure and that she was going to embrace this one.

She lifted her phone and pulled up her dictionary app—she was always puzzled when people were surprised she used it so often. Why wouldn't you take advantage of having a dictionary at your fingertips?

Thanks to being in the middle of nowhere, it took forever for her phone to spit out the definition.

ad·ven·ture *noun*

an unusual and exciting, typically hazardous experience or activity

"Wait. Typically hazardous?" Jemma's voice pitched higher. "Why didn't I read this definition *before* moving here? Señor Fluffypants, did you know about this?"

Her bunny stuck his furry head out from under the couch, but the loud bang on the door made him skitter back underneath. It also made Jemma jump enough that she dropped her phone. She stared at the wooden door as if she had X-ray vision.

Who'd come knocking when she didn't know anyone yet? Especially in this storm?

The loud rapping noise came again, and there was something odd about it. It sounded low and almost...metallic?

Jemma gripped her phone in case she needed to call the cops—who knew how long it would take them to get all the way out here?—and padded across the room. There wasn't a peephole because of course there wasn't.

She swung open the door, and a large horse snout darted inside.

She fell back on her bum, her mind struggling to make sense of the image in front of her as her tailbone throbbed from the impact. The falling sleet around the white horse served as a dreary background, and the creature whinnied, the sound even louder than the raging storm.

"I'm not sure what you want," she said, because this had been a weird day and she might as well cap it off by talking to a horse.

The horse stomped a foot, the metallic cling of its shoes making her go *ah, that was why the knock sounded like that.* It didn't magically tell her why there was a horse on her porch, though.

Just how backwoods was this town?

Jemma pushed to her feet and cautiously approached the horse.

The cold air was rushing in, making her wish for the blanket she'd left on the couch, but when the horse sniffed her hand, she couldn't bring herself to pull away and slam the door in its face. He—or she—was beautiful. White, all except the black nose and gray speckles across its face. Sleek and muscular, with a long, snowy mane blowing in the wind.

Out of the corner of her eye, Jemma caught movement, and a dark figure materialized as whoever it was strode closer. More details stood out as he stepped into the pool of light the open door sent across the porch.

Male, tall, strong jaw, and cowboy hat.

Read the rest! Country Hearts *is available now.*